Rafe took a deep breath. "Julie, marry me."

That got her attention. "Are you crazy?"

"Yes. It doesn't have to be a forever thing. It doesn't have to be a romantic thing. But let's get married so that the babies will have the best start we can give them."

She raised her brows. "Marrying you is a best start?"

"Yes. I know you don't have a whole lot of reasons to trust me right now, but we need to do this for the children."

"Not really. And don't start with the father's-last-name machismo. Jenkins is a fine name, a better name in this town than Callahan."

Dear Reader,

Valentine's Day is such a romantic day—a bright spot in cold February! For Rafe Callahan, romance was always a no-go with the beautiful Judge Julie Jenkins, his next-door neighbor and the bane of his existence. He found himself in quite a fix, falling for the one woman he knew he could never have—Julie simply didn't think much of footloose, handsome Rafe. In Julie's opinion, the man totally deserved the fifty red hearts she drew on his face while he was asleep—a practical joke his brothers heartily endorsed! But it seems that waking up covered in red ink was just the beginning, and somehow, sweet Valentine *triplets* were the next big surprise Julie had for the sexy cowboy!

I hope you enjoy this fourth book in the Callahan Cowboys series. It's my great wish that *His Valentine Triplets* will add happiness and romance to your reading during this special season!

All my best,

Tina Leonard

www.tinaleonard.com

www.facebook.com/tinaleonardbooks

www.twitter.com/tina_leonard

His Valentine Triplets

TINA LEONARD

TORONTO NEW YORK LONDON
AMSTERDAM PARIS SYDNEY HAMBURG
STOCKHOLM ATHENS TOKYO MILAN MADRID
PRAGUE WARSAW BUDAPEST AUCKLAND

Recycling programs
for this product may
not exist in your area.

ISBN-13: 978-0-373-75389-5

HIS VALENTINE TRIPLETS

Copyright © 2012 by Tina Leonard

This edition published by arrangement with Harlequin Books S.A.

For questions and comments about the quality of this book
please contact us at Customer_eCare@Harlequin.ca

www.Harlequin.com

Printed in U.S.A.

ABOUT THE AUTHOR

Tina Leonard is a bestselling author of more than forty projects, including a popular thirteen-book miniseries for Harlequin American Romance. Her books have made the Waldenbooks, Ingram and Nielsen BookScan bestseller lists. Tina feels she has been blessed with a fertile imagination and quick typing skills, excellent editors and a family who loves her career. Born on a military base, she lived in many states before eventually marrying the boy who did her crayon printing for her in the first grade. Tina believes happy endings are a wonderful part of a good life. You can visit her at www.tinaleonard.com.

Books by Tina Leonard

HARLEQUIN AMERICAN ROMANCE

**Cowboys by the Dozen
*The Tulips Saloon
‡The Morgan Men
†Callahan Cowboys

There are so many people I can never thank enough for the success in my writing career, but at the top of the list are my patient editor, Kathleen Scheibling; the magical cast of dozens at Harlequin who unstintingly shape the final product; my family, who are simply my rock; and the readers who have my sincere thanks for supporting my work with such amazing generosity and enthusiasm. Thank you.

Chapter One

"Rafe is too smart for his own good."
—Molly Callahan, recognizing the seeds of mayhem in
her too-bright toddler

As Augusts in New Mexico went, it was a hot one. Rafe Callahan stared at Judge Julie Jenkins in her black robe in the Diablo courtroom and felt a bit of an itch. Was it the heat, or was he just thinking about what they'd done in July when his steer had gotten tangled in her fence?

"Counsel," Julie snapped to his brother, Sam. "Why should I recuse myself from hearing *State* v. *Callahan?* Have you any substantive reason to assume that I could not hear proceedings in this matter fairly?"

"Judge Jenkins," Sam said deferentially, "as you know, your father, Bode Jenkins, has brought suit against our ranch, invoking the law of eminent domain."

"Not my father," Julie said, her tone stiff. "The State handles matters of eminent domain."

Yeah, Rafe thought, *and everyone but Julie seems to understand that her father is in it up to his neck with every government official and thief in the local and state governments. Good ol' Dad can never do anything wrong in his little girl's eyes, and vice versa.*

Julie's gaze flashed to him, then away. *Guilt.* It was written all over her beautiful face. He knew what was under that prim black robe, and it was the stuff of dreams, a body made for the gods. He'd been lucky enough to find the chink in her sturdy armor—a testament to the fact that she couldn't resist him, Rafe thought smugly.

He'd made her guilty. Julie knew very well that their night together meant she should step down from this case.

"Mr. Callahan," Julie said to Sam, after sending another defensive glare Rafe's way, "it seems to me that you have no good reason why I shouldn't hear *State* v. *Rancho Diablo*."

Sam, the crack-the-whip attorney assigned to saving the Callahan family fortunes, looked down at his notes, marshaling his thoughts. It was important that Julie not be the judge hearing this case, Rafe knew—as did all six Callahan brothers—because she was completely partial to her father. What good daughter would not be? But Julie seemed to have it in her mind that the case was purely New Mexico versus the Callahans, not Jenkins versus Callahans, Hatfield and McCoy style.

Ah, but he knew how to bring little Miss Straitlaced to heel. He hated to do it. She'd been a sweet love that one night, and a virgin, which wasn't so much a shock as it had been a pleasure he'd remember forever. He got warm all over, and stiff where he shouldn't be at the moment. There was something about those brown eyes and midnight hair that just undid him, never mind that she had enough sass in her to send up fireworks.

But this was war, unfortunately, and the Callahans needed all the help they could get to draw level with Bode Jenkins and his bag of crafty tricks. Rafe stood, and with Julie's gaze clapped on him warily, leaned over to whisper to Sam. He could feel her eyes on him, as well as those of his brothers, his aunt Fiona and uncle Burke's, and half the town, who'd come to hear today's proceedings. Julie wouldn't want to be embarrassed in front of the people who'd helped raise her after her mother died. But it had to be done.

So he whispered some nonsense in Sam's ear about the price of pork bellies, all the while knowing that Julie thought he was telling Sam about their passion-filled sexcapade.

"Now act surprised," he said to Sam, and his brother pasted a dramatic and appropriately shocked expression on his face.

Julie said quickly, "Would counsel step up, please?"

Sam went to Julie, as did the lawyer for the State, a slick Bode yes-man if Rafe had ever seen one.

"I'll consider recusing myself," Rafe heard Julie say, her tone soft yet tinged with anger. His ear stretched out a foot trying to hear every word. "But I'm not happy that you've indicated I don't hear cases completely fairly. I've never been asked to recuse myself before, and I feel this is another case of Callahan manipulation, for which they are famous."

Her accusing stare landed on Rafe, and he couldn't help himself. He grinned. She stiffened, so cute in her judge getup, but completely naked to his eyes. It was as if she knew it.

After a long glare his way, during which time he noted her pink cheeks, and her full lips pressed flat with annoyance, she said, "Court will adjourn while I consider the motion. We will resume in one hour. And Mr. Callahan," she said, her voice tight as she addressed Rafe, "I'd like to speak with you in my chambers, please. Counsel will not be required."

"You've done it now," Sam said in a low voice. "She's going to eat you alive, scales and all. It's your fault, too, for sitting there smirking at her."

"I can't help it," Rafe said. "She just looks so stiff and formal in that robe. I remember tacking her hair to her desk in biology class, and chasing her on the playground. It's hard for me to take her seriously."

"She's going to teach you the meaning of respect, dude. Good luck. I'm off to get a hot dog." Sam sauntered away, his conscience clear, unconcerned about his brother's impending misfortune.

Rafe sighed and approached the chamber of doom. "Judge?"

"Come in, please, Mr. Callahan, and close the door."

She sounded like a vinegary old schoolteacher. Rafe sat down, and tried to arrange his face into the most respectful expression he possessed.

"Mr. Callahan," Julie began, and he automatically said, "You can call me Rafe. I'm not a formal guy."

She nodded. "As you wish. And you can call me Judge Jenkins."

He nodded, reminding himself not to grin at her prissy tone. The fact was, Julie was in command of their futures at Rancho Diablo. If they could get her to recuse herself, they could probably get a more impartial judge to hear their case. This thought alone kept Rafe from smiling. He even tried his damnedest not to stare at Julie's legs, shapely stems skimmed by the black robe, and elongated by high-heeled black pumps. Very severe, and very sexy. She wore her ebony hair in a no-nonsense upsweep, which made her look like a dark-eyed, exotic princess. She wore a lipstick that was a shade off red, and he wanted to kiss her lips until there was no lipstick left on her.

But he couldn't. So he waited for her ire to recede.

"Mr. Callahan," she began again, "you may be under the misapprehension that because we have had an engagement of a personal nature—"

"Sex," he said.

Her full lips pursed for a moment. "You may be under a misapprehension that I will tolerate disrespect in my court."

"No, Judge. I have the utmost respect for you."

Her big brown eyes blinked. "Then quit smiling at me in the courtroom, please. You look like a wolf, which you may not be aware of, and it comes across as if you take this proceeding lightly."

"I do not." Rafe shook his head. "Trust me when I tell you that this proceeding is life-and-death to me."

She nodded. "See that you try to maintain a more serious composure in the courtroom."

"I will." He nodded in turn, his expression as earnest as he could make it. "And you're wrong, Julie. Just because I let you seduce me in a field doesn't mean I don't respect you."

She gasped. "I did not seduce you!"

He shrugged. "You're a powerful woman, Julie. Not only are you beautiful and smart, you're sexy as hell. I couldn't resist you." He shook his head regretfully. "Ever since then, I've wondered if holding you in my arms was a dream."

She glared at him. "You can be certain that I didn't seduce you. You—you…" She seemed at a loss for words for once. "You seduced *me!*" she said in a whispered hiss. "This is what I'm talking about, Rafe. You Callahans always manage to twist things around!"

"Oh, Judge, it's every man's dream to be seduced by a gorgeous woman. Don't burst my bubble." Rafe smiled his most charming smile. "I wish I could seduce you, but I'm pretty sure you're impervious to men."

She blinked. "That didn't sound very nice."

"Maybe you're just impervious to me." He sat on her desk and swung a leg, considering his words. "That's probably it."

"I don't even know how that happened that night. But," Julie said, her voice low, "I'd appreciate you not bringing it up again, and particularly not in the courthouse."

"But was it good for you?" Rafe asked. "That's a worry that's kept me up at night."

Julie drew back. He gave her a forlorn look. "Good for me?" she repeated.

He nodded. "Did I make you feel good?"

She hesitated. "I guess so. I mean, considering it was you, I guess it felt as good as it could have."

He tried not to laugh. She was lying like a rug, and in her own judge chambers, just down the hall from where she made people take oaths to tell the truth. "Ah, Julie," he said, "there are nights when I wake up in a sweat thinking about how sweet you are."

She appeared confused. Probably no one had ever said that to her before. But he knew she was sweet. He took her hand and tugged her close to him. "Seduce me again, Julie."

"No," she said. "You're bad news, Rafe Callahan. My dad always says that, and it's true. You're really, really bad, and I should never have—"

He touched his lips to hers, stopping her words. "So why did you?"

"I don't know," she said, not pulling away from him. "I have no idea why I even let you talk to me, Rafe. I shouldn't have done it, though, and I can tell you it will never happen again."

"I know." Rafe framed her face with his hands. "And it makes me so damn sad I just don't know what to do." He kissed her gently, then with more thoroughness as he felt some of the stiffness go out of her. "We geeks never get the beautiful girls."

She blinked, pulling back. "Geeks?"

"Yeah. You know, those of us who think too much, when we should be men of action." He moved his hands down her shoulders, down her arms, and began kissing along her neck. God, she smelled good. He had a stiff one of epic proportions sitting in his jeans, and the call of the wild firing his blood. "I'm guilty of thinking too much, when I should be going after what I want."

He circled her waist, holding her to him, and kissed the hollow of her throat.

"Rafe—"

"Mmm?"

"Is this about the court case?"

He pulled back a moment. "Is what about the court case?"

"This."

He looked into her dark eyes, completely confused. His mind was totally fogged by Julie, her sweet perfume, her sexy mouth—and then he realized what she was asking. "God, no, love. I compartmentalize much better than that." He couldn't help the grin that split his face. "I may be a thinker, but I'm not that good, sweetie. This is all about trying to get under the robe of the most beautiful girl in Diablo."

Julie seemed to consider his words. Rafe was pretty certain he should strike while the iron was hot. Clearly, she was of two minds about letting him kiss her, and the fact was, he wasn't about to let Julie out of his grasp. He remembered far too well how wonderful it had felt to be inside her. So he did what any normal, red-blooded man would do when faced with an uncertain female: he staked his flag on Venus. Pushing up Julie's robe and dress and everything else that was in his way, he slid off the desk and kissed her soft tummy. She gasped, and he ran his hands under her buttocks.

"What are these?" he asked, staring at the darling little pink straps holding up her stockings. Julie looked like a Victorian saloon girl, and he was pretty certain he was so hard right now diamonds couldn't chip him.

"Garters," Julie said. "And a thong."

"Pretty," Rafe said, and moved the thong so that he could kiss her the way he wanted to. Gently, he licked and kissed and tasted her, and when her knees were about to buckle, he pushed her into her desk chair where he could kiss her to his heart's content. He'd waited a long time for this moment, and when he could tell she was about to rip his hair out by the roots, he licked inside her, taking great pleasure in her gasping cries as she climaxed.

He wanted to just sit and look at her for a second, all disheveled in her black robe, but she shocked him by grabbing his belt. "Wait," he said, "just a minute, Julie. I don't want you to do anything you don't—"

She cut off his words with urgent kisses. Okay, he wanted her to do everything. She was pulling at him, trading places with him, and the next thing Rafe knew, he was sitting in the tall-backed black leather chair and Julie was sliding down him, clutching his shoulders as if she was afraid he was going to disappear.

What could he do but give her exactly what she wanted? "Hang on," he said, crushing her bare buttocks in his hands so that he could hold her tightly to him. He thought he was going to black out from the pleasure. Julie gasped against his neck, then tore off the judge's robe and threw it on the floor.

"Let me help you." Rafe undid the frilly white blouse she had on, tossing it away. That left a sweet ivory bra, but he was a pro with bras, and he had that hanging over a law book before Julie could realize that she now was seated on him wearing nothing but a soft peach skirt, pink garters and black heels. *I'm living a dream,* Rafe thought, taking in Julie's breasts, which were beautiful, shapely, peach-nippled. He wanted to grab them, but his hands were full of her soft buttocks and he had her right where he wanted her, so when she rose on a thrust and wrapped her arms around his neck, and her breasts engulfed his face, he was profoundly grateful. He sucked in a nipple before it could get away, and Julie stiffened on him, giving him a very pleasurable jolt where it counted.

"Oh, Rafe," she murmured. "Oh, God, don't stop."

He didn't. He suckled, and thrust, and touched, and invaded. And when Julie tightened up on him, giving a tiny muffled shriek of pleasure as she came, Rafe held on for just a moment longer, making sure he'd never forget this moment, before letting himself surrender to the magic of Julie.

He was pretty certain he'd rested his case, and that the jury had found him more than irresistible.

TEN MINUTES LATER, RAFE tried to help Julie dress.

"I've got it, thanks." She swept his hands away, fixing her robe and her skirt. He could tell she didn't want to meet his gaze, so he pushed his white shirt into his dress jeans and straightened his tie.

Tidied up, Julie regained her professional demeanor. "This is awkward."

"Not really." Rafe stole another kiss, which he noticed she didn't return. Well, of course, she needed time to process how much she wanted him. He grinned. "See you in court."

Julie didn't smile. "Remember, please. Respect, Mr. Callahan."

"Oh, I do, Judge." Taking her hand, he raised it to his lips. "I respect the hell out of you."

She jerked away. Rafe saluted her and went to the door. Then he turned, catching her eyeing his butt just before she realized he'd found her staring. "Next time, this is going to happen in a bed."

Her cheeks pinked. "There won't be a next time."

He smiled at her. "The thing is, as good as it is between us in all these hot locations you pick out, Julie, I could make you feel so much better in a private place where I can spend hours giving you pleasure you'd never forget."

She gasped. "Go!"

He nodded, drinking in her straight posture with appreciation. She was a darling little thing, so prim and bad by turns. My God, he loved a woman with sass, one who said no but begged so prettily, too. He didn't tell her that her hair was slightly mussed—actually, she looked like a Barbie doll that had gotten caught in a windstorm—and he didn't tell her that her lipstick was shot. Nor did he tell her that somehow she'd forgotten to put her bra back on. It was still draped over a law book in the corner of her office.

"Thank you, Julie," he said softly, meaning every word, and then he left her chambers and returned to sit beside Sam.

"Where the hell have you been?" his brother demanded. "I brought you a hot dog."

"Thanks. I'm starved."

"So, did she read you the riot act?"

"Pretty much." Rafe bit into the cold hot dog, moaning with satisfaction.

"Did you apologize for pissing her off?"

"I did. I apologized the only way I know how. Is this soda for me?"

Sam nodded. "And did she accept your apology?"

"She did. She accepted everything." Rafe chewed his hot dog happily, feeling like a new man, thanks to his encounter with Julie. "She's a very generous woman."

"I'll say she's generous if she accepted your dopey apology." Sam sighed. "I hope you didn't do anything to change her mind about recusing herself."

Rafe froze. "Uh…"

Julie swept into the courtroom. Everyone rose as the bailiff instructed, then seated themselves again. Rafe swept his food out of sight.

"She doesn't look happy," Sam said.

No, but she does look satisfied. His little judge was going to flip when she realized she'd forgotten to put on lipstick. Her hair was pretty much blown out of its 'do. She looked gorgeous to him, but flustered, and Rafe grinned, thinking that next time he wasn't kissing Julie Jenkins until she begged him to.

He snapped himself out of his sexual reverie, realizing that her gaze was on him, and she did, in fact, look annoyed again. It was the smile, he remembered, and he put on his most serious expression.

She didn't seem impressed.

But she had been a few moments ago, and that had to speak well for the future. He hoped so, anyway. *Next time, I'm going to figure out how those little garter things work, and spend about an hour kissing the judge where I know she likes being kissed the most.*

"THOUGH THERE IS NO fundamental reason for me to recuse myself," Julie said, "I will do as the defendants have requested. Let the record reflect that I do so with a good deal of misgiving for the request that was made of this court." She pinned Rafe and Sam with a mutinous glare. "Court adjourned."

"She's really ticked," Sam observed. "This will not be good for our neighborly relations."

Rafe watched Julie sweep from the courtroom on a cloud of displeasure and irritation—with maybe a little embarrassment thrown in. He watched her go, fascinated by the woman he loved wrapped in a real good snit. What Julie didn't know was that he loved her all the more for her spiciness and warmth, and now that she was good and mad at him, he was dedicated to getting her out of that black robe again. He had a one-track mind when he wanted something, and he wanted Judge Julie Jenkins badly.

They said the best sex was makeup sex—and if that was true, then he was all for making up as soon as humanly possible.

"THAT WAS UGLY," SAM SAID as he and Rafe walked out into the sunlight. People left the courthouse and were milling around, chatting over what had happened in Julie's court.

"Not ugly," Rafe said, thinking about how beautiful she was. "The Callahans are free to fight another day."

His brother shoved his briefcase into the front seat of his truck. "I'd like to know what Judge Julie was thinking that made her do a turnaround like that. She is not an easy judge to sway. Frankly, I was expecting a lot more fight. And what the hell was all that 'act surprised about pork bellies' crap? We don't do pork at Rancho Diablo."

Rafe shook his head. "It doesn't matter now." He got in the passenger seat and pondered how he might ever put his plan of The Seduction of Julie into place. As Sam had said, she was not an easy woman to sway—and she seemed to hold him in as much esteem as a rattlesnake.

If he didn't know better, he would think she hadn't enjoyed his lovemaking.

But he did know better. Judge Julie didn't have a faking bone in her body, and the woman put on no grand act. He'd be forever thankful for his steer getting tangled in her fence in the first place. Okay, maybe making love in a field on a blanket he'd grabbed from his truck wasn't a woman's idea of My First Time, but by golly, he'd waited for years to hold Julie Jenkins, and he'd made the most of it. He'd had her sighing and moaning like crazy, a yearning cat under his fingertips. Today, he'd tried to make her second time something she'd remember with a heaping helping of must-have-more. "I'd just put it up to the fact that she'd heard of your reputation, bro, and went down before the fight."

Sam shook his head. "There's something funny about Judge Julie calling uncle that easily. Bode's hired one of the best teams of lawyers around."

Rafe clapped his brother on the back. "No one's as good as a Callahan."

And it's true, Rafe thought. *I've had it from Judge Julie's own lips. Maybe not in those exact words. Maybe not in any words at all. But I know Julie Jenkins digs her some Callahan cowboy.*

FOR A WEEK, ALL WAS SILENT. Rafe saw his brothers at mealtimes and at work, and everybody seemed preoccupied. He wrote it off to the heat. Jonas was moody, but what the heck. When one was a retired surgeon turned rancher, perhaps one got moody. Jonas had always been a brooding cuss, anyway, and as far as Rafe could tell, his oldest brother had been eyeing Sabrina McKinley for the past couple of years, and nothing had changed. If there was one thing guaranteed to put a man off-kilter, it was the unrequited desire for the love of a good woman. It could kill a guy. "Or at least the lust for a good woman," Rafe amended out loud, earning a glance from Sam, who was studying a mass of papers almost as thick as the Bible. Rafe went back to considering the sales figures for Rancho Diablo, but his mind wasn't on it. *Sam works too hard. He's been trying to save this ranch for nearly three years now, and I don't think he's even looked at a woman in all that time. Callahans should have it easier getting sex than we do.*

"The problem," Rafe said out loud, "is that we all work too hard. And we're picky."

"What, ass?" Sam said. "Do you mind taking your braying elsewhere? These briefs are eating me, and I can't think with you chattering like a teenage girl."

His brother definitely needed a woman. "You know,

Sam," Rafe said, "since I'm the thinker of the family, I've been thinking. And I think it's time we got you out of the house."

Sam glared at him. "Thank you, Sophocles, for that bit of news I can't use."

"Dude, this lawsuit has sucked you dry."

"You have a solution?" Sam shrugged. "I'm not giving up on Rancho Diablo, no matter what barrel Bode Jenkins thinks he's got us over."

"Yeah." Rafe considered his brother. "Nothing seems to be working, does it? Aunt Fiona's Plan has gone off the rails. We've had weddings and babies out the wazoo around here, and our brothers have populated a small town all by themselves, and still we can't convince the courts that we should have our own zip code free of Jenkins."

"Do you mind, Hippocrates? Can I get back to this?" Sam waved some documents.

Rafe grunted. "I'm just saying maybe you ought to get some fresh air. Or get lucky, alternatively, if that's in the range of your possibilities."

Sam laughed, and it wasn't a pretty sound. "And when, pray tell, was the last time a woman opened her door for you, Einstein?"

Rafe couldn't brag. It would make Sam feel bad. He probably felt that they were brothers in bachelorhood. Of the six Callahan boys, only Sam, Rafe and Jonas were unmarried. No woman was going to throw her cap at Jonas, because he was about as much fun as a wart. Sam had an easygoing style, when he let himself hang loose, which wasn't often.

Of the three of them would-be champions to Fiona's Plan to get all the Callahans married—and then award Rancho Diablo to the brother with the largest family—Rafe figured he had the best chance. *I have the highest IQ, I have the best hair, I fly the family plane and girls love geeky guys like me.*

"If you knew anything at all about Hippocrates, brother, you would know that he believed the body must be treated as a whole and not just a series of parts. Therefore, with your mind in overload over Rancho Diablo's attempt to free itself from Bode Jenkins, you're under too much stress. We've got to find you a woman."

"Excuse me," Sam said, "but I didn't hear you tell me when you last saw a woman naked and welcoming you."

Rafe didn't reply. He didn't want Sam to feel bad, and he would never let the cat out of the bag about the judge. Especially since Sam was pitting his wits against Julie's father.

"That's what I thought, genius." Sam went back to glaring at the mountain of paper in front of him.

"Never say I didn't try to help," Rafe stated, and leaned back to continue studying ranch paperwork.

The bunkhouse door blew open with the speed of a rocket, crashing against the wall. Rafe's jaw sagged as Bode Jenkins barreled into the room.

The old rancher was holding a rifle in his hands, pointing it at him.

"Jesus, Bode," Sam said. "Put that popgun down before someone gets hurt."

"I'm going to *kill* him," Bode said, glaring at Rafe. "You dirty, thieving dog!"

"Are you talking to me?" Rafe stood, pushing Sam behind him. "What the hell, Bode?"

Fiona burst in behind their neighbor and faced him, before kicking him a smart one on the shin. "Bode, give me that gun, and cool your head. Whatever's gotten up your nose now, it isn't worth doing time in jail."

Burke appeared and snatched the gun from Bode, who seemed to give it up without much fight. All the other Callahans filed in, glaring at the rancher, then glancing around the room to make certain everyone was in one piece.

"Do you mind telling us what's going on?" Jonas demanded.

"I'll tell you," Bode said, his voice quavering. The man's face was red, pinched with fury as he glared at Rafe.

"No, you won't." Julie winked and shoved a few Callahans out of the way so she could reach her father. "Dad, you're going to give yourself a heart attack. Calm down."

Rafe blinked at Julie, who was stunning in a summery sundress and sandals, with her inky hair swept up in a ponytail. There was just something about her that hit him like a fist to the solar plexus every time he saw her. He liked her in her judge's robe, he liked her in a dress, and he loved her naked in the moonlight.

But something had her wound up tight. More than the court case. "What's up?" he asked her. "What's got Bode steamed this time?"

That got Julie's laserlike attention. She practically stabbed him with her eyes as she sent him a particularly poisonous glare. "Now is *not* a good time for you to be speaking disrespectfully to my father. I just saved you from being shot, Mr. Callahan, so if you don't mind, zip your lips."

Well, wasn't that a big dose of judgelike attitude? He grinned at Julie. She liked him, he could tell. No woman was that starchy around a man unless he rattled her love cage. He couldn't wipe the smile off his face.

"Bode, the next time you come running onto our property like a madman—and may I remind you this is not the first time you've acted crazy…" Fiona began.

Bode pinwheeled his arms with frustration. "You Callahans make me crazy. Why can't you just git? This is my land, my property, but you're like fleas. You multiply like fleas—"

His face turned redder, as if he'd just thought of something horrific. He glared at all of them, reserving his most potent fury for Rafe. "You—"

"Dad," Julie said, "we're leaving right now. Come on. There's nothing here we want."

Rafe watched her go, tugging her protesting father along with her. Of course there was plenty here Bode wanted. He wanted the ranch, he wanted their home, he wanted the Diablos and the rumored silver mine—

Bode whirled, punching his finger toward Rafe as he escaped his daughter's clutches. "You're not winning," he told him. "You haven't won."

Julie dragged her dad from the bunkhouse.

"Damn," Rafe said, "I believe Bode's finally gone over the edge." He sank onto the leather sofa. His brothers and Fiona and Burke gathered around. "I thought he had a caretaker over there to keep an eye on him."

"Seton's busy, I think," Fiona said. "She's been over here helping Sabrina with some things for me." Their aunt shrugged. "Seton does have time off, and she chooses to be here with her sister. That has nothing to do with Bode's visit, because he seemed mostly upset with you." Fiona looked at Rafe. "Didn't he say he was going to kill you?"

Rafe shrugged in turn. "I took that 'you' in the global sense, as in all of us. I don't think he meant me personally. If he wants to kill anyone, it would probably be Sam, who is beating him all to hell in court."

"Oh." Fiona nodded.

"I swear," Rafe said. "I didn't do anything to the old man. We all agreed we'd abide by the law, and the decision of the courts, and I'm cool with that." He held up two fingers in a V. "Peace, brothers. It's all chill in the house of Callahan."

Jonas snorted. "Yo, thinker, don't do anything stupid. The man is tense, and next time we might not be around to save you."

"Save me?" Rafe shook his head. "He's crazy. Everyone knows it."

"Everyone may know it, but that won't save you if Bode decides to get crazy on you."

Burke looked at Fiona. "Actually, that's the most upset I've ever seen our neighbor. Thankfully, his firearm wasn't loaded, although they say there's really no such thing as an unloaded gun."

"He *is* crazy," Fiona agreed, "but he'd been quiet for a while. Which made me nervous in a different way. But now I'm really nervous." She looked around the room at all the brothers. "Now is as good a time as any to tell them," she said to Burke, and Rafe thought, *oh, that didn't sound good.*

"It's up to you," Burke said, moving his hands to her shoulders.

Fiona looked down, allowing Burke to massage her shoulders, which was strange, for this independent woman rarely accepted anyone's comfort. Rafe could tell his little aunt was struggling to put her thoughts in order. Bode's untimely visit had put speed to something that had been on her mind. Rafe waited, feeling tense himself now.

"Burke and I believe that Bode's ill feelings in this suit have largely been directed at me. I've been a thorn in his side for quite some time," she said.

The room was so silent Rafe thought he could hear Sam's heart beating beside him, which was really annoying. *It should be my heart I hear beating. Sam's always been one for attention. It's why he's a lawyer.*

"Remember the Plan I put forth to all of you? How I put Rancho Diablo in trust for whichever of you married and had the largest family?"

They all nodded. A couple of his brothers looked pretty proud, because they figured they were in the lead. Rafe snorted. It didn't matter. They'd decided among themselves

that, whoever won it, they were going to divide ranch ownership between them equally, in spite of Fiona's Plan. And once
he got started making a family—when he finally decided
to settle down—Rafe would make all his brothers look like
beginners, anyway. There was such a thing as proper planning, which all men of deep thought knew. Strategy. Chess
players understood the importance of strategy, for example.

"Well, after a great deal of thought, worry, prayer and
yes, even strategic plotting, Burke and I have decided," Aunt
Fiona said, taking a deep breath, "to move back to Ireland."

Chapter Two

"Now see what you've done, brain man," Sam said beside him, and Rafe turned.

"What?" he demanded. "What did I do?"

"You've upset Fiona." Sam shook his head. "None of this would have happened if you hadn't ticked off Bode and his precious pumpkin, Julie. By the way, did you get my play on words? Brain man? Like the movie *Rain Man?*"

"Yeah, a laugh riot." Rafe turned to face his aunt. "Okay, before everything gets really out of hand, I suggest we discuss topics of concern that affect the ranch and its future." He went to Fiona and patted her on the back. "Let's meet in the library in thirty minutes, which will give everyone time to finish what he was doing just as our neighbor had another of his dramatic fits."

The brothers went off in separate directions, muttering and murmuring. Rafe looked down at Fiona. "It's going to be all right. You can't let Bode upset you every time he decides to be a clown. Because he does it so often."

She stared up at him, her eyes bright. "I've made a lot of mistakes, I know, in my raising of you boys and the management of this ranch. But I cannot let something bad happen to any of you." Fat tears plopped down Fiona's wrinkled cheeks.

He hugged her. "We're grown men, Aunt. You don't have to worry about us anymore."

"That's not what that rifle said." She sniffled.

"Yeah, but we all know Bode's a terrible shot."

"Eventually even a bad shot finds a mark."

That might be true. Rafe pondered the wisdom in his aunt's words as he held her to him. He looked at Burke over Fiona's head. The only father figure most of the brothers remembered shrugged helplessly.

"All right, no more tears. We'll get this figured out." Rafe patted Fiona on the back and let Burke lead her away.

She was shaken, of course. They all were. Except him, for some reason. *Staring down the barrel of that gun didn't upset me like it should have.*

Bode was just superhot under the collar because the Callahans made his precious lamb recuse herself from the lawsuit. He'd expected Judge Julie to be his ace in the hole.

Ha.

"Crazy old man," Rafe muttered under his breath.

But an annoyed Jenkins was not to be treated lightly. Rafe remembered the time Julie had been teed off with him, and his brothers had let her into the bunkhouse where he'd been sleeping off a bender, and she'd drawn about fifty tiny red hearts all over his face with indelible marker. It had taken a week for those suckers to wear off. He'd been the laughingstock of Diablo.

He still had a bone to pick with her about that.

She hadn't looked too happy with her father's attempt to put a piece of lead in him today, but it wasn't because she cared what happened to Rafe. All Julie cared about was her old man.

"Which means," Rafe muttered as he left the bunkhouse to head to the family council, "that the next time we make love, I'm going to have to make certain that the folks all the way over in Texas hear my darling little judge banging her gavel as I completely disorder her sweet little court."

"YOU REALIZE HE'S AN ASS," Julie Jenkins snapped to Seton McKinley thirty minutes later, after she'd remanded an exhausted Bode back into Seton's care.

The blonde and beautiful care provider blinked at her. "Your father?"

"No," Bode interrupted, impatient for the story delay. "Rafe Callahan. He's an ass. An eight-point horned ass."

Julie sighed. "Dad, calm down. Put all this behind you. Most importantly, it's against the law to go waving rifles at people and threatening them. I know you don't realize this, but you jeopardize my career when you lose control."

"I would never do that."

Bode looked at her with big eyes. Julie sighed again, realizing only too well how much the Callahans got under her father's skin. "Dad, you did. I could be in trouble for not calling the sheriff out on you."

"This is what I'm talking about." Bode waved a hand at her and Seton. "The Callahans are always at the root of every problem."

"Usually I agree with you wholeheartedly." Most especially, she would agree with him that Rafe was something of a rascal. No sooner had his longhorn gotten caught on her land then Rafe had shone all his legendary Callahan charm on her. And she, like a weak, silly princess in a fairy tale, had let him wake her up from her self-imposed sleep, and then made certain she'd not had a night since when her dreams weren't interrupted by his devilishly handsome, always grinning face. She didn't even want to think about what he'd done to her last week in her own chambers—and yet she hadn't had five minutes where she didn't remember his mouth all over her body, tasting her hungrily as if he'd never had a meal so good. It sent shivers shooting all over her just thinking about it.

"This time, I can't agree with you. You're at the root of this problem." Julie settled a red-and-black plaid blanket over her father and left him to Seton, who seemed to have decent luck soothing Bode. Once again the situation was equally split, with blame for both sides. Her father was angry that the Callahans had asked her to recuse herself, and the Callahans were doing what they had to do to keep their ranch. It was all pointless. In the end, Bode would get Rancho Diablo. Her father always got what he wanted.

She should have taken herself off the case long ago. But she'd wanted to stay in control as long as possible to make certain the Callahans didn't pull any of their numerous tricks on her father.

Callahans were famous for practical jokes on people they considered friends, and dirty tricks on those they didn't.

She had to protect her dad.

"I gave him a shot of brandy, and he went right to sleep." Seton walked into the kitchen and handed a glass to Julie.

"Oh, no, thank you." She waved away the crystal glass and reached for water.

"I'm not sure what set him off," Seton said. "I'm sorry I wasn't here when he got emotional."

Julie shook her head and began unloading the dishwasher. "Trust me, there wasn't anything you could have done. When Dad gets his mind made up, off he goes. Wild horses couldn't hold him back."

"Do you know what was bothering him?"

Julie didn't turn around. "The Callahans. They always bother him," she said simply, but she knew the truth wasn't simple at all. "Don't worry about it, Seton. Dad gets worked up about once a month. It always blows over."

"All right. Let me know if you need anything."

She nodded, and heard Seton leave the kitchen after a moment. Julie kept straightening, her mind not really on the task. After she finished the dishes, she closed the dishwasher and went out to the den to look at the black-and-white photos on the mantel. Almost every picture was of her and Bode. Riding horses. Swinging on the porch swing. Hunting deer. Skiing in Albuquerque. She'd framed them all in black frames so they matched, a chronology of their years together. Just the two of them—except one photo.

That picture was of her, Bode and her mother. The three of them, a family, before Janet Jenkins had passed away from cancer. Bode had been a different person before her mother died. He was pretty focused now on wheeling and dealing, the thrill of the hunt.

Julie didn't think her father had ever mentioned the Callahans except in passing before he'd become a widower. His hatred of that family knew no bounds now.

Of course, the Callahans stirred the pot like mad. Fiona was no wimp at plotting herself, and seemed to take particular delight in keeping Bode wound up.

Julie had gotten revenge once, but even when drawing hearts all over Rafe's face, she'd known she was totally attracted to him. Like his twin, Creed, he was lean and tall, with dark hair and a chiseled face. Creed's nose looked a bit broken, but Rafe's certainly wasn't, despite the fact he'd rodeoed and been in numerous fights. He was totally, hauntingly masculine. Julie couldn't touch his skin and not know he was totally delicious.

But she'd never dreamed she'd slip under his spell and willingly shed her dress and her inhibitions for him—cross line, father and court to experience the wonder of making love with Rafe Callahan.

"He's still a jackass," she muttered. Rafe did not like her. She was pretty certain their day in court had been a game, a Callahan hookup, for which the cowboys were famous. She looked at the picture of herself as a small child held by her mother, and knew there were some things she couldn't even tell her father. He was just too mentally fragile these days—and some things were too terrible to confess.

Especially when they had to do with Callahans.

Unfortunately, she was pretty certain she was under the spell of a certain black-haired, crazy cowboy.

"THERE IS NO REASON for us to pay any more attention to Bode than we have before," Rafe said. He looked at Fiona, who was seated next to Burke in the upstairs library. Each brother had joined in the family council to discuss the next move, and Fiona's startling pronouncement.

Rafe took a sip of brandy from a crystal glass. "The strain of the suit is no doubt taking a toll on everyone, but there's no reason for you to feel that you're the problem, Aunt Fiona." He shrugged. "Bode's just getting himself caught in his own game, and it's making him a little nutty."

"That's right," Jonas said. "There's no reason for you to go back to Ireland, when we need you here."

"I second that," Pete said. "Who would watch my three bundles of joy? Jackie needs help now more than ever."

"I third that," Creed said. "I've got my hands full with *kinder* now that Aberdeen's expecting again. Her sister Diane living on the ranch with Sidney means three more toddlers on top of that. Who has the energy to keep up with all these children besides you, Aunt Fiona?"

She gave them all a leery glance. "Do not try to entice me with babies."

"But that was The Plan all along, wasn't it?" Judah grinned. "The Plan was to get us married and in the family way as quickly as possible. You wanted babies, and we complied."

"And have been having a lot of fun doing it," Pete said, and everyone booed him.

"It's true, though." Creed glanced around at his unwed brothers with a big grin. "The fifty percent of you who haven't joined in Fiona's Grand Plan don't know what you're missing out on."

Rafe rolled his eyes. "Dirty diapers? Sleepless nights? Pint-size potties?"

Creed raised his glass. "Nightly lovemaking that you don't have to go hunting for."

"Afternoon quickies on call," Pete said with a smile.

"Booty that has your name on it," Judah said with a big grin, "and furthermore, has her name on yours, as much as you can stand it."

Rafe blinked. "Jeez. Is it all about sex with you knuckleheads?"

"Yes," his three married brothers said in unison, and Rafe sighed.

He knew exactly how they felt. If he could go home to Julie every night, he'd beg her to cook naked for him. He'd make certain she had see-through baby doll nighties that he could tear off her every night, a different one for every day of the month. He'd—

Damn. They're getting to me. My own brothers.

He looked at everyone staring at him, and swallowed hard. *Creeps.*

"Anyway, what I was saying before I was so rudely interrupted," Rafe said with a glare for the married side of the room, "is that if you leave, Aunt Fiona, you cede the field to Jenkins."

"Which is a bad idea," Judah said, "because you've been running Rancho Diablo for over twenty years. There's no reason for you to let him run you off."

"And besides," Pete chimed in, "someone's got to marry

off the rest of our brothers. We don't need half of us causing trouble in our bachelor phases."

"Jonas, Sam and Rafe." Creed shook his head. "My twin, Rafe, and Jonas, the eldest of the bunch, and Sam, the youngest of the bunch. I'd say we still need you, Aunt Fiona."

"Don't coddle me," she said. "Don't try to lure me with babies and matchmaking and spitting in Bode's eye. I know what's best, and what's best is that Burke and I leave you men to unite against a common foe."

They all stared at their tiny, determined matriarch.

"Damn," Rafe said, "that's pretty strategic thinking, Aunt."

She nodded. "One of my better plots, I must say."

He glanced around the large library. His brothers lounged in various positions, some looking lazy (but always ready for action), some rumpled (hard workers), and Jonas, who looked cranky, as always.

Rafe loved his brothers. They were a tight-knit band.

"But what if we don't unite?" he asked. "What if we turn on each other?"

"Would you?" Fiona asked, looking at him.

"Hell, I don't know. There's a ranch at stake." He shrugged. "Without your hand on the reins, we might go running wild through the New Mexico desert."

"I doubt it." Fiona's voice was crisp. "Anyway, today's flare-up has convinced Burke and me of what we'd been discussing since Bode launched his grab for your land. We think you are better off without me here to rile him. I've divided the ranch up into six equal parts. For the three of you who are married, I've put your portion in your name. For those of you who are not married, your portion is in trust, which you will receive upon my death or your marriage, whichever comes first. Without me here, I'd say it won't be marriage."

She nodded and took Burke's hand. "It has been an honor to raise you. We love you like our own sons. We always did. There are a lot of questions you may one day want to ask, and when you're ready, we'll answer them for you. And remember that everything you think you know isn't always what is. Take good care of each other, and most importantly, be brothers."

Fiona and Burke made their way from the library. Rafe tried not to gawk at the departing figures of their aunt and uncle. "I think she's serious."

Sam nodded. "She really believes she's the source of Bode's anger. I say we just kill him."

They all snorted at him.

"She can't go back to Ireland," Jonas said. "We need her here. She belongs here. Burke belongs here. They haven't been back to Ireland in over twenty-some years. What are they going to do there?"

The brothers turned to stare at him.

"That is the most emotion I think I've ever heard you spew," Rafe said. "I feel like I'm in the presence of the angel of human psyche."

"There's probably no such thing," Sam said, "but that *was* pretty heavy, Jonas, for a tight-ass like you."

Jonas threw a tissue box at them. "Go ahead, bawl your brains out. We all want to."

"I'm not crying." Rafe took a deep breath, not about to let himself get drizzly, although he did feel like a water balloon in danger of being punctured. Fiona's decision had left him pretty torn up. "I'm going to convince Fiona she's worried over nothing. I'm—"

They heard a door slam. The brothers glanced at each other.

"Must be going out to check on the horses," Creed offered.

"Or to change her holiday lights. It's about time for her to take down the Fourth of July décor-anza." Pete nodded. "She left them extra long because all the little girlies liked them so much. She said her great-nieces should always have sparkly decorations to look at."

Fiona was famous far and wide for her lighting displays. Rancho Diablo always looked like a fairyland, sometimes draped with white lights, sometimes colored—but always beautiful. "I want to wring Bode's scrawny chicken neck," Rafe said.

"I do, too," Judah said, "but that'll just land us in jail."

"Miserable old fart." Rafe couldn't believe what had happened. His luscious Julie had to know that her father was beginning to go around the bend. Not that she would ever admit to such a failing in him, locked in her ivory tower of daddy-knows-best. "Maybe Bode has terminal dumb-ass disea…" Rafe stopped, listening to a sound that had caught his attention. "Was that a motor? A vehicular motor? Visitors, perhaps?"

Or Bode serving up more trouble.

The brothers looked at each other, then jumped to the many windows of the library to study the driveway in the dimming evening light.

"*That* is a taxi," Jonas said, "and if I'm not mistaken, our aunt and uncle just bailed on us."

Chapter Three

"I'm not sure what any of this means," Sam said to Rafe a week later. They were all busy trying to adjust to Fiona and Burke's sudden departure. He waved a bunch of legal documents. "It seems our aunt was keeping a lot of secrets."

Rafe gazed out toward the horizon of Rancho Diablo. The two of them were in Fiona's library, Sam having called him there to vent his frustration with their aunt's dispensation of the ranch. "You'll figure it all out."

"I wish I'd known half the stuff before we got knee-deep in battling Bode. Did you know that originally this land was owned by a tribe? Our father bought it from them."

Rafe shrugged. "That explains the yearly visit from the chief, maybe."

"Yeah, it sure does. The tribe retained the mineral rights to the property."

Sam sure had his full attention now. Rafe turned away from the window to goggle at his brother. "All mineral rights?"

"Oil, gas, silver—you name it, it's not Rancho Diablo's."

Rafe couldn't help grinning.

"What's so damn funny, Einstein?" Sam snapped.

"Bode doesn't know." Rafe laughed out loud.

After a moment, the thundercloud lifted from Sam's brow. "That's right, he doesn't. And he can't sue a tribe for their mineral rights. Well, I guess he could, but he wouldn't win. This is a signed and properly executed document."

They both sank onto a leather sofa and chuckled some more. Jonas poked his head in, favoring each of them with a grumpy gaze.

"Don't you two ever do any work?" he snapped.

"Listen, Oscar the Grouch, close the door," Sam told his elder brother.

Jonas obliged, though not happily. "Why are you two lounging when there's work to be done?"

Sam handed him the sheaf of papers. Jonas gave it a cursory glance and handed the stack back. "I don't have time to read a wad of papers as thick as your head. That's your job, Counselor."

"Well, if you would read," Sam said, "and if you could read, as your medical degree claims you can, according to these papers, Rancho Diablo Holdings owns no mineral rights. They are instead owned by the tribe of Indians from which Chief Running Bear hails." Sam grinned, waving the papers. "An interesting turn of events, don't you think?"

Jonas stared at his brothers with obvious disbelief. "All mineral rights?"

"Yep. All we own is the land and the bunkhouses and the main house. Actually, if you think about it," Sam said, waxing enthusiastic about the topic, "no one really owns the houses, either. The banks do, and even once they're paid off, the government can still come along and decide to kick you out. They either want the land for building, or they decide you owe back taxes on the property, and poof! There goes your domicile." Sam shrugged. "The value is in the mineral rights, I'd say, and those, brothers, we do not own."

"And we never did," Rafe said, glancing at the papers. "These documents were executed the year before you were born, Sam."

"Yeah, I noticed that." He frowned a bit. "But let's not go there for the moment."

"Holy Christmas," Jonas said, "that means Bode's lawsuit is basically nullified."

"In large part, if not in total," Sam agreed. "Lovely day, don't you think?"

"Fiona knew this," Jonas said. "She had to know the mineral rights weren't ours, and that we couldn't give them over even if Bode won his case."

"Maybe she didn't," Rafe said, wanting to defend their small, spare aunt. "Even Sam said he didn't really understand the papers."

"I understand them perfectly," Sam said, "and I can't find any documents that state otherwise, which might indicate a later sale from the tribe to Rancho Diablo Holdings. So what that tells me—"

"Is that Fiona probably never saw those documents," Rafe said stubbornly. "They were signed before she came. When our parents were alive."

Sam pursed his lips. Jonas sighed and looked out the same window that Rafe had been gazing from. Rafe knew his brothers thought Fiona had withheld the information on purpose.

"She hardly had time to go digging through every document pertaining to the ranch. Overnight, she became guardian to six boys in a foreign country," he pointed out. It made him slightly angry that his brothers seemed to think Fiona might have been deceptive about what she knew about their property. She was the executor of their estate. "It doesn't make sense."

"She became guardian overnight to five boys," Sam said, bringing up a point that Rafe had chosen to gloss over. "I came later."

Rafe saw no reason to chase that particular ghost right

now. He waved a dismissive hand. "You're a Callahan. Let's not dig up every screaming specter in this house right now."

"What I'm saying is that Fiona knows who my parents are," Sam said, and Rafe and Jonas stared at him in shock.

In all the years they'd been a family, this was the most they'd discussed Sam's abrupt arrival. They wouldn't have even known about it, but Jonas had been old enough to remember that Sam had come later—after the accident that had claimed their parents. Rafe wished Fiona hadn't left, and that all this discussion of documents had never arisen. Nothing good could come of the past interrupting the present. He looked at Sam's strained face and felt sorry for his brother.

"I'm just saying this because Fiona knows who my parents are, and she knew about the mineral rights. I know that," Sam said, "because Chief Running Bear doesn't swing by every Christmas Eve just to share toddies with our aunt in the basement."

"Well, he probably does," Jonas said, "if I know Fiona."

Rafe sighed. "This is ridiculous. Just call her and ask. Or go down to the county courthouse and sift through some records. There's no point in getting all wild and woolly about stuff that doesn't matter." He felt ornery at this point. It was too hard seeing Sam suffer. "There'd be no reason for her to keep this from us," he said, refusing to believe that their aunt could be quite so manipulative. "If she'd known, she would have revealed it in court so Bode would shove off."

Jonas shook his head. "She might be protecting the tribe."

"Or she didn't know!" Rafe insisted.

"Or, and this is the most likely scenario," Sam said, "this was the perfect way to get right up Bode's nose."

Rafe blinked. "You mean to let him sue us for practically no reason?"

Sam shrugged. "Everyone's been talking for years about

the rumored silver mine on our property. We know there's nothing here, but Bode would believe the gossip. More important than land would be a silver mine. Treasure seekers have always tilted at windmills."

"Bah," Rafe said impatiently. "So what. I'll tell him myself." He was getting more ruffled by the moment, which made sense, since he was enamored of making love with Bode's daughter.

"You can't tell him," Jonas said, his tone forceful and big-brother-like for a change. "None of us in this room is going to say a word to our brothers or anyone, until we find out why Fiona didn't want it known that the mineral rights had been sold. I'm pretty certain it's bad to withhold pertinent information in a court case, and we can't get our aunt in trouble."

"Not in this case," Sam said. "Fiona and Burke are just going to say that the document was executed before they arrived, and they had no knowledge of its existence. And you," he said to Rafe, "may I suggest you curtail your activities with a certain judge? Try not to annoy her or her father? We need time to figure everything out, before we hurt our case or our aunt. And I don't trust you to keep your mouth shut if you're in the throes of pleasure."

Rafe crammed his hands in his pockets so he wouldn't take a swing at his brother, and told himself that the family that kept secrets together stayed together.

He could keep a secret.

He could stay away from Julie.

No, I can't.

I'm sitting on a powder keg. And when it blows, I'm probably going straight to hell.

LIFE DIDN'T SEEM TO BE getting any better when Rafe opened the door to his room in the bunkhouse and found the judge sitting on his bed. "What the hell?" he asked, trying to be nonchalant and not quite making it. She looked delicious, and as heat flooded his groin he realized he'd never been cut out for a monklike existence. "Get out," he said. "If you've come to mess up my face with a permanent marker again, I should warn you I don't fall for the same tricks twice." He waved his hat at her. "Anyway, let's go out in the main room."

"I have to see you privately," Julie said, and Rafe sighed.

If it was up to him, he'd love to see the good judge very privately. But he wasn't going to break with the rules set forth by his brothers, even if the rules were unfair as hell. He looked at Julie's clouds of luscious dark hair and beautiful tilted brows and delectable full lips and made himself sound stern. "Julie, you need to go."

"Rafe, I'm not going."

"Then *I'll* go." He turned to leave, and it was harder than leaving behind part of his own body. He told himself he was truly a man of steel for his virtuousness.

"Rafe," Julie said, standing up, "we have to talk."

But his brothers had warned him, and somewhere in his mind, he figured they were probably right. "You'll find me on the couch if you want to tal—"

Her hand on his arm stopped him. "Rafe."

Well, technically, they were in a doorway; they weren't really alone, right? "Yes?"

"If I have to have this discussion with you via a court order, I will."

He grunted. "So your father sent you."

"No one sent me. I'm here because I need to talk to you." She looked at him closely. "The last two times I've seen you, you've done your best to seduce me, and unfortunately, I've let you. Now you're acting like you don't even want to look at me…" Her voice drifted off. "It *was* all about the lawsuit."

He blinked. "What was?"

"Seducing me in chambers. You just wanted to convince me—compromise me—into recusing myself."

"Well," he said, wishing he could kiss her, but knowing he couldn't without risking his brothers' wrath, "it's an interesting premise, but no."

She pulled away from him, standing a prim and proper three feet away, no longer in the doorway but outside in the den. Rafe knew it was for the best, though he could tell by the hurt look on Julie's face that she completely had the wrong impression.

But how could he tell her that if it was up to him, he'd toss her into his bed right now and ravish her until next week?

He couldn't. And the curse of it was he'd never had Julie in a bed. Never had her with hours to spare.

Always quickies. "Damn."

"What?" Julie stared at him, her pretty face wreathed with suspicion.

"Nothing," Rafe said with a sigh. "Anyway, what did you want to tell me?"

She took a long look at him. "I wanted to tell you I heard through the grapevine that your Aunt Fiona and Uncle Burke have left."

He shrugged. "It's true. What of it?"

"What does this mean for the lawsuit?"

He shrugged again, not interested in discussing it. "Ask your father."

"I…we don't discuss it much," Julie said, and Rafe snorted.

"Right. You were the judge in charge of hearing the case."

"And since I'm off the case," Julie said with heat, "we have not discussed it, or your family. I am not the judge, and therefore I am not privy to details!"

She was so cute when she got snippy.

"You're a jerk," she said, when he made no reply, and she flounced out the door, her white sundress practically blinding him as he tried to stare through it. He remembered her delightful derriere, and he wanted her. She made him crazy in ways he'd never been crazy before.

"I am a jerk," he said, and turning, bumped into Sam.

"I won't argue with that," his brother said gleefully. "I heard the whole thing, and you have very little understanding of how to treat a woman, bro."

"What the hell does that mean?" Rafe snapped, his patience addled by being so near Julie and unable to possess her. "You told me to stay away from her until this whole thing blows up or over."

"True," he conceded, "but she didn't wear that darling little dress to talk about cases, dummy. She came wearing that hot number hoping you'd take it off of her." His grin was wide. "Boy, are you dumb."

Sam continued on, and Rafe sighed before heading out to the barn.

He wasn't dumb. He was playing it safe, and right now, that seemed like the smart thing to do.

And maybe the only thing to do.

RAFE CALLAHAN WAS AN ASS, Julie fumed as she stalked to her truck. She got inside and resisted the urge to peel out of the Rancho Diablo driveway. It would solve nothing, and it served no purpose for him to think he'd won.

That's what this was all about. From time immemorial, women had been played by Romeos, and she was no different. The Callahans were great tricksters, fond of practical jokes and mayhem. They loved one-upping anyone who tried to outdo them.

Her father was right: Callahans were trouble. And she

should have known better than to think there was anything real going on between her and Rafe.

"An ass," she muttered. "A big, braying ass."

Her heart jumped and fluttered as she thought about how wonderfully he kissed, and she wiped at a tear that slid down her cheek. One tear, that was all she'd spare for that tall, dark, handsome Romeo.

He wasn't worth her time.

Unfortunately, she still had to talk to him. The problem now was telling him what she had to tell him without killing him.

This time, she wouldn't settle for permanent marker hearts all over his face.

A branding iron would be much better, but unfortunately, she didn't have one of those. "Oh, heck," Julie said to herself. "This is not going to be good."

Chapter Four

"So," Jonas said, rattling pots and pans in the kitchen as Sam walked in. "We're going to need to organize KP duties. I think an org chart might be necessary. We'll divide up days of the week for cooking, cleaning—"

"Whoa," Rafe said, "I'm not eating your cooking."

"Excellent," Jonas said. "You can have my days."

"All right," Rafe said, as Sam entered the kitchen and poked his head in the fridge. "You can do my cleanup."

"Why can't we just eat out?" Sam asked, his face mournful as he considered the fridge. "Frankly, I don't think the three of us are qualified to take care of ourselves."

It was probably true. Creed, Pete and Judah had wives and families who could take care of them. Rafe figured Jonas and Sam were pretty useless at providing for themselves, and he didn't particularly want to be shackled with babying them. Sabrina lived upstairs at the main house, but she definitely could fend for herself. Rafe grimaced. He could take care of himself, too, but someone was going to have to take care of his boob brothers. Sam was busy with the court case and probably couldn't subsist on hamburgers from Banger's Bait and Tackle, not if they wanted him firing on all cylinders legally. And Jonas didn't have the sense to come in out of the rain. Rafe sighed as he looked at his helpless brothers. "We could hire a cook."

"For the three of us?" Jonas looked outraged. "Doesn't that seem wasteful?"

"It seems practical," Rafe snapped. "I make good food, but I'm not cooking for you babies."

They both looked at him with regret in their eyes. Rafe realized that a trap had been sprung on him. "You two discussed this. You planned this pity party! You want me to do the woman's work—"

"Don't let a female hear you talking that way," Sam interrupted with a glance toward the ceiling, as if he suspected Sabrina might be lurking upstairs. "You'll get your head handed to you."

"I don't care." He shot his brothers a sour look. "What a pair of wienies."

"If you cook," Jonas said, "I'll do the grocery shopping."

"And I'll do cleanup," Sam said. "Sort of. We'll eat off paper plates and use paper napkins. No more niceties like cloth napkins, which Fiona used to spoil us with." A woeful sigh escaped him.

"And what about clean sheets in the bunkhouse?" Rafe asked. "Basic hygiene? We haven't taken care of ourselves our whole lives."

"No time like the present," Sam said, injecting cheer into his tone.

Rafe wasn't buying it. "We need a housekeeper. Jonas, you're going to have to open the purse strings."

"I can't," he stated. "Remember, we said we were going to be cautious with our resources until the lawsuit gets dismissed."

Crap, Rafe thought. "If I cook it, you eat it, no whining. And I never, ever do cleanup." The very fact that his brothers had shanghaied him into this, when he needed to be thinking about Julie and her long, beautiful legs, teed him off greatly. "I do not have time to be Rachael Ray for you lazy bums. But I will, as long as all I ever hear from you is 'mmm-mmm good.'"

"Deal," Jonas and Sam both said, and Rafe stalked out of the kitchen, wondering why today was his day to have everyone lined up against him.

He poked his head back inside the kitchen. "Starting tomorrow."

His brothers nodded eagerly.

"By the way," Jonas said, "congratulations."

Rafe blinked. "On what? Being a patsy?"

Jonas stared at him for a long moment. "Yeah. Sort of."

"Great. Thanks." Rafe left again, wondering why Jonas had looked so surprised. "Jerk," he muttered under his breath, though he loved his older brother. The word *jerk* made him think about Julie calling him that, walking away from him in her pretty white dress, and he decided maybe thinking about her was just too hard.

To hell with his brothers. They were weird, anyway, even for Callahans.

He was the last normal one left on the range.

FIVE MINUTES LATER, RAFE stared at Julie's latest handiwork in the bunkhouse. As pranks went, it was a doozy. He appreciated the size and scope of her one-upmanship. He hadn't wanted to pay attention to her, so she clearly had decided there were better ways to get a man's attention.

She'd put a sign on his bedroom door in the bunkhouse. It had a stork carrying a blue-swaddled bundle of joy.

His breath stung in his chest. "'Congratulations,'" he read aloud, "'baby Jenkins arrives in May. Julie.'"

Rafe was reeling. There'd been no warning. No clue.

Except from Jonas, but whoever paid attention to him?

"My world has gone mad," Rafe muttered, and tore the stork off his door.

He was not having a baby. This was some mad attempt by Julie to rattle him, like the time she'd doodled on his face. Only this would last longer than a week. His brothers would be in top form over this joke. Everyone knew that Callahans were supposed to marry and populate. She was adding fuel to the fire.

But the sign said May. That was pretty darn definitive, and judges were typically pretty careful with details. Rafe tried to take another gulp of air and decided he might be having a wee panic attack. He needed a shot of something stiffening, like perhaps whiskey.

He hit the bar, and didn't bother with a glass, just let the liquor burn down his throat from the bottle. After capping it, he wiped his brow and concentrated on the pain.

"I had no other way to tell you," Julie said, stepping out of his room. Rafe's throat went dry as a bone, no longer moist from the alcoholic drenching. "It takes a lot to get your attention, cowboy."

"There's no way," he told her. "I used a condom when we were in the field. Mind you, it wasn't the newest, but latex lasts forever. It's nuclear material. So you must be mistaken, Julie. Condoms are safe."

"I don't remember hearing the sound of foil tearing open in my office."

This was true. "I figured you were on the pill or something by then," he said, and Julie looked outraged.

"Excuse me if I never considered us an ongoing thing."

He blinked. "And now?"

"Now you know." She walked past him, obviously about to leave. "That's all I owe you, Rafe."

"Who else knows?" he asked, wondering if he needed to talk to Bode.

"You and whoever saw this sign."

"Did Jonas know you were waiting in my room?" Rafe's head was spinning. "I mean, he told me congratulations."

She smiled. "I asked him not to."

Great. Everyone loved pulling the wool over good ol' Rafe's eyes, he thought bitterly. "Well, things will have to change. You, me, everything."

"Probably," she said, and walked out the door.

As if he was supposed to know what to make of that. Rafe hurried after her. Julie got in her truck, gunning it, sending up plumes of driveway dust, and the little judge went off without even a glance at him.

Not even caring that she'd totally kicked his ass in a major way.

"I'm going to be a dad," Rafe said. "More importantly, I'm also going to be a husband, whether that little judge and I ever see eye to eye on the subject or not."

"Talk to yourself often?" Sam asked, wandering by with a smirk on his face. "Dad?"

"Only when I want to," Rafe said, and headed off to ponder what the hell had just happened to him.

"YOU'D BEST FIND A BUNKER," Jonas told Rafe an hour later when he found him staring up at the ceiling, his gaze fixed on the plaster as he lay on the leather sofa. "Bode's going to tear you limb from limb when he hears the not-so-good news. Jeez, Rafe, what were you thinking?"

"I wasn't."

"Obviously. This throws a wrench into everything."

"Tell me about it," Rafe said. "Great sex goes out the window once the little woman's got a bun in the oven. And I never got to have great sex with her." He moaned piteously.

"Ugh," Jonas said under his breath to Sam, who leaned over the sofa to punch his brother in the chest with a grin. "Do something with him, will you? Explain to him how neatly, with one fell swoop, he's destroyed our court case you've slaved over for three years."

"Idiot," Sam told Rafe. "You're supposed to be the smart one. Turns out you're the dumbest of all." He laughed, enjoying his brother's plight.

"It's not funny," Rafe said. "Now she hates me."

"Now we all hate you, dummy." Jonas sank onto the sofa, staring at the fireplace. "I was hoping it wasn't true. I was hoping you weren't as dumb as you look. Once again, however, you prove yourself."

Rafe waved a hand in the air. "Try being me for a change. The most beautiful woman in the world is having your baby. She doesn't want you. Life is ugly from where I'm lying."

"Please don't let me ever be that pitiful," Jonas said aloud. "If I ever get like him, Sam, you're in charge of shooting me."

Sam took a seat in a wingback chair. "It's just that he's been convinced for so long that he was so much smarter than everyone. Bulletproof, like Superman. Only now you're Superwienie," he told Rafe. "This is going to complicate the hell out of things, especially when Bode comes to kill you."

"I know," Rafe said. "I think I better go talk to him."

"No!" Sam and Jonas exclaimed.

"Don't set a foot on that property, Rafe." Jonas's tone was grim. "Don't go see Julie. Don't upset Bode. We'll try to hide you as best we can, but we're not the Secret Service. We're not nannies, damn it."

"Be careful," Rafe said. "I'm the cook. Mind your manners or you'll be eating Rice Krispies for days."

Sam shook his head. "Look, Plato, Jonas is right. You're going to have to lie low. If you think Bode wanted to put lead in you for picking on his little girl when we made her recuse, he's going to send out a team of snipers to take you out once he finds out you've knocked up his little lambkins."

"I think he should leave town," Jonas said, as if Rafe wasn't there. "He could hit the rodeo circuit. The boys'd cover for him. He could fly the plane up to Alaska and do something productive for a change."

"Fly fishing's productive?" Rafe asked. "I'm not going anywhere except over to Julie's."

"No!" Sam said. "Look, freak, you're in big trouble, even if you're too dumb to know it. God, all kinds of IQ and not a grain of street smarts."

"I'm going to handle this like a man." Rafe jackknifed to a sitting position. "I'm not going to run like a cowardly dog."

"You're going to go until this clears over." Jonas glanced at his watch. "Right now, only the three of us and Julie knows. But she can't keep her secret long. So pick a place and get gone. We don't have time to baby you to death."

"You could go to Ireland to check on Fiona and Burke," Sam said.

"Hell, I don't care if he goes to Mars," Jonas said with a growl. "I just want him where he can't cause more trouble."

"The tribe might hide him," Sam suggested, and Rafe jumped to his feet.

"I'm going," he said, mashing his hat onto his head.

"Where?" his brothers demanded.

"To Julie's. Where else?" Rafe strode out the door.

"Just a warning," Seton McKinley said, as she helped Julie carry some groceries into the house. "Word around Rancho Diablo is that when a Callahan decides he wants a woman, he's pretty unshakable in his determination."

"It won't matter to me." Julie set the grocery bags on the counter in the big, white kitchen. "You just take care of Dad, and I'll handle Rafe Callahan. And if you tell a single soul, even Sabrina—"

"I won't." Seton pushed food around in the fridge. "Don't

say I didn't tell you, though. How do you think your father would like spaghetti for dinner? Or I could grill some hamburgers."

Julie glanced upward. "Did you hear something?"

"No." Seton looked at her. "But your father is napping, so it's probably just a creak in the ceiling."

Julie frowned. "Maybe I should check on him."

"I will." Seton left the kitchen, and Julie sank into a chair.

She was going to have to tell her father. It was probably going to kill him. The worst thing she could ever imagine was becoming pregnant by her father's worst enemy.

"I am a horrible daughter," she murmured out loud.

"He's fine," Seton said, coming back into the kitchen. "Are you all right?" She looked at her, concerned.

"I'm fine. I think." Julie felt cold, almost sick with nerves.

"You don't look fine. You look like you just ate a bad oyster." She put away the groceries Julie had left unattended. "It's going to be all right, Julie."

"You don't know Dad. The shock could—"

"Nope," Seton said, interrupting her worrying. "He's a tough guy, Julie. Nothing can kill him."

"You didn't see him after my mother died. His skin turned gray," Julie said quietly. "I thought I was going to lose him. And he's not as young as he used to be."

Seton sat down across from her. "So what are you going to do?"

Julie didn't answer. She thought about her dad, and how he would take the news. He was a proud man. Of course he would feel that the Callahans had won, that they'd done this on purpose. That there'd been a plan to get her pregnant, so that Bode would drop the suit. Everyone knew Fiona had a Grand Plan to get her nephews wives and lots of babies so community sentiment—and pressure—would be on their side. Fiona wanted Bode to look like a bad guy, an evil man.

He wasn't.

"I thought I just heard something," Seton said, glancing at the ceiling as Julie had. "Like a thump."

She shook her head. "I'm going to go take a nap."

"Good." Seton rose. "I'll start dinner. Don't worry so much, Julie. It isn't good for the baby."

Julie blinked. "Don't talk to me about babies. Not today. Maybe tomorrow."

She went upstairs, remembering the shock on Rafe's face. He'd seemed thunderstruck, although not angry, not upset, not unhappy. Just thunderstruck. As she'd been, when she went to the doctor's complaining of some nausea, and discovered she was pregnant.

She'd never even thought about becoming a mother. And now she was going to be one.

Closing her bedroom door behind her, she walked straight into her bathroom. Pulled her hair down, looked at her pale face. Seton was right; she did look as if she'd eaten something bad.

A nap would soothe her. She went to crawl into her four-poster bed with the white lace hangings—and stopped dead in her tracks seeing the long, lean cowboy lounging in her bed, sound asleep.

"Oh, for a good indelible marker right now," Julie said, and whapped Rafe with a pillow.

Chapter Five

Rafe put his hands up to protect himself from the pillow assailing him.

"Have you no respect? No fear of my father?" Julie demanded. "No shame, Rafe Callahan, at stealing into my bedroom and falling asleep in my bed?"

He was relieved when she quit whaling him. "Let's see. No, I have no fear of your father, thanks for asking. Shame? Nope, I'm pretty low on that, too. After all, you've stolen into *my* bedroom, Julie Jenkins."

"Get out or I'll scream."

"Nah," he said, loving the sudden high color in her cheeks. "You're not a screamer, love, except maybe in bed. We'll have to investigate that. I kind of think you are." He smiled at her, knowing he was making her madder.

"You're a rat." She stared at him, highly annoyed, but not throwing his boots at him. They lay on the floor at her feet, right where he'd dropped them as he got into the marshmallow-soft bed, and he took that as an excellent sign.

"You're a cad, a bad man, a—"

"I get the picture." Rafe held up a hand. "You don't like me. And yet you do. What a complete conundrum for you, a quandary, even."

Julie began smacking him with the pillow again. "I don't even know what you're saying half the time," she complained. "I think you make stuff up—" she hit him again, harder, though the goose down wasn't making much impact "—because you have a big stupid head and think you're smart, and—"

He grabbed her wrist and pulled her into the bed. She fell with an ungraceful *oomph!* and he buried his lips in her hair. "I told you I'd eventually get you into a bed, Julie Jenkins."

"Not *my* bed," she said, trying to hop out, but he held her fast to him.

"Go to sleep. We have a lot to talk about, and we can't talk when you're cranky and worked up like this, darling."

She kicked back and caught him a smart one on the shin.

"That's going to leave a big bruise," he said, rueful but not letting go. "I hope you locked the bedroom door."

"I did not," she said, her voice tight as a guitar string. "When my father finds you in here, he's going to—"

"Shh." Rafe ran a hand through her long hair, as he'd wanted to do for so long. "You need your beauty sleep, lamb chop." He felt safe teasing her because she'd dropped her pillow and was lying fairly still now. Tense, but still.

She talked a hard game, but she was a softie for him.

"You fall asleep in my bed again, Callahan, and you won't ever wake up."

He laughed, pulled her tightly against him so her derriere was right where he wanted it, and promptly dozed off.

WHEN JULIE AWAKENED FROM the best rest she'd had since learning she was pregnant, she was shocked—then annoyed—to find herself alone in her bed. *Typical. Sneak into my bed and then sneak back out.*

Something was going to have to be done about the father of her child. "He can't be an arrogant male 24/7," she muttered, smoothing her hair to go downstairs. If he thought he was just going to move in and take over her life now that they were expecting a child together, he had a surprise coming.

"Seton," she said as she walked into the kitchen, "that smells delicious."

"Thank you," Seton said.

"Do we have a large nail?"

Spoon in hand, Seton turned to her. "How large? To hang a big picture?"

"To nail a window shut."

Seton's eyes widened. "The thumping noise we heard was your window?"

"It was boots hitting the floor after a big cowboy climbed through my window. Apparently he doesn't use front doors." Julie smiled. "I'd like to teach him that climbing trees to sneak in windows is dangerous."

Seton put down her spoon. "I'll go get a hammer and the largest nail I can find in the toolshed."

"Thank you." Julie began humming as she went to her office to study some law books for existing statutes on a new case she was hearing.

The nerve of that man to think he's above the law—

Although Rafe did have a point: Like everyone else, she treated the bunkhouse as if it had a Welcome, We're Open sign on it.

No more, she resolved. She'd paid the last visit to Rafe that she ever would—and they were never, ever sleeping together again.

"I THINK," JONAS SAID as the three brothers ate a few pre-made burgers they threw on the grill that night, "we're screwed, thanks to you, Romeo."

"It looks grim," Rafe admitted, though he didn't feel grim. Knowing he was going to be a father made his heart sing with joy. If there was ever a time to praise the joys of condomless sex, this was it. His brothers could rib him all they liked, but Julie was his.

And all thanks to his good ol' sex appeal and charm.

"I just wonder when she's going to tell Bode." Sam threw his burned bun in the trash with disgust and stared up at the velvety sky. "You're still alive, so he hasn't heard. Doesn't your gut cramp just a little, knowing you're soon to be a dead man?"

Rafe shrugged. "He's a bad shot. Besides, Julie talks a tough game, but she wouldn't let anything happen to me. She's really into me."

"Oh, for crying out loud." Jonas shook his head and sank onto the redwood bench near the grill. "Did you ever once think about the ranch? Or just yourself?"

"At the moment that it all occurred," Rafe said, "I was pretty much just thinking about how good it felt, and how long I'd waited, and how lucky I was, and—"

"Would you shut up?" Sam glared at him. "You're nauseating."

"Why?" Rafe glanced around at his brothers. "I'm crazy about the woman. I have been for years. Sure, Bode's going to be a little wound up when she tells him, but it's nothing we can't handle."

"We?" Jonas stared at him. "We?"

"We, the ranch. Isn't that what you're all worried about?"

His brothers looked at him.

Sam sighed. "No common sense at all." He poured a half gallon of ketchup on his bun to drown the charred edges, and took a bite. "Are you going to marry Julie or not?"

"Marry her?" Rafe blinked. "I never thought about it."

Jonas spewed out his beer. "Do you want your ass kicked? Of course you're going to marry her!"

"I mean," Rafe said patiently, "she wouldn't marry me. She's going to have to understand that, as the father, I have certain rights. I will be staying with her every night, for example. It's my right to protect her and my baby, and provide for them financially." He shrugged. "Marriage is like a mirage to me right now. Far in the distance, pretty much just a figment of imagination where Julie is concerned. I'm lucky if she talks to me."

He was sad about that. Secretly, he wasn't certain how long he could keep up Robin Hooding through her window. Breaking down her walls. Scaling her tower and all that rot. "It's hard romancing a woman," Rafe said, "especially one who's as independent as Julie."

"If Aunt Fiona was here, she'd whip you into shape, you sad sack," Sam said. "I'm almost embarrassed you're my brother. And you're older than me. You should be setting a good example."

Rafe wasn't certain what his brothers wanted from him. They didn't realize that to get Julie to acknowledge him, he needed a dark room and thirty minutes. The woman had never said hi to him on the Diablo streets. She'd cross the road to avoid him. "You don't understand. As far as Julie is concerned, the Callahans are rodents."

They sat at the picnic table, considering that.

"I'm doing the best I can," Rafe assured his brothers.

"Do better," Jonas said. "This isn't even about the ranch. It's about your future child, who's going to wonder why his daddy lives on the next ranch over and didn't marry his mother."

Rafe sat very still, his mind envisioning the scenario.

"I could sue for custody," he said, and Sam let out a hiss.

"She's a well-respected judge, dummy. No other judge in this county or beyond is going to take her child from her and give her to you, a guy who has no common sense." Sam drank from his beer bottle and regarded him. "I don't know how you'll get out of this mess."

Rafe shook his head. "Me, neither."

"You really don't have a plan, do you?" Jonas asked.

"If I had a plan, I'd be over there eating real food with my woman instead of sitting here listening to you two wheeze." Rafe got up and threw his untouched burger into the trash. "It would be so much easier if women just did what we wanted them to do."

"Sounds like a real romantic guy," Sam said, and Jonas said, "Sounds like a guy who's going to get a woman real mad." They went off, leaving Rafe sitting at the picnic table.

He looked up at the New Mexico night sky and thought about teaching the constellations to his son. Playing football, riding rodeo. Looking for the Diablos.

Julie can't leave me out of her life. Somehow, our two lives have got to meet in the middle.

He just didn't know how they could.

A WEEK LATER, RAFE FOUND himself dragged off by Seton and Sabrina McKinley for a private chat in the north barn. Being surrounded by beautiful blondes was not a bad thing, but since he had a not-too-chatty raven-haired beauty on the brain, he wasn't in the mood to be corralled.

Still, he sank onto a hay bale and tried to look attentive. "So, what can I help you ladies with?" he asked.

Seton gave him a once-over. "It's more like what we can help you with."

Sabrina nodded. "We debated whether we wanted to have this conversation with you. We feel like traitors. So please keep our visit to yourself."

"Who are we hiding from?" Rafe asked. "You guys live upstairs, when you're not over at Bode's. It's hard to hide anything around Rancho Diablo."

"We don't want you telling Julie that we talked to you."

Sabrina looked at him. "She's not too happy with you right now."

"She'll get over it," Rafe said. "She'll have to."

"She's nailed her bedroom windows shut." Seton gave him a sidelong glance. "I don't think she plans to get happy with you anytime soon."

Rafe leaned back on the hay bale and tried to act as if he wasn't concerned. He was, but man law required saving face. "So what's up?"

"Since your aunt Fiona left, we've been in a small situation. You're the one we chose to talk to about it. Fiona always said we could trust you," Seton said, "and that you were the smart one who could think your way out of any box."

"It's true," Rafe said with a deliberate lack of humility for the praise. "I like puzzles."

Seton perched on an old cracked leather chair and stared at him. Her sister parked nearby against a saddle rack. "So, the first thing you should know is that your aunt hired us to do some work for her."

Rafe waved a hand. "Yes, cooking and cleaning is very important at the ranch."

Sabrina rolled her eyes. "I told you he could be a wee bit dense for a smart guy."

Seton nodded. "Dense is perhaps too mild a word. Look, cowboy, I'm a private investigator and Sabrina is an investigative reporter."

"When she's not telling fortunes." Rafe smirked. "Wasn't that how you came to Rancho Diablo in the first place? To warn us that our ranch was in trouble? If I recall correctly, your sister was posing as a gypsy from the circus."

"Which your aunt hired her to do. Pay attention, Rafe. I can't be gone too long from Mr. Jenkins. He doesn't know I'm here." Seton looked irritated, so Rafe sat up and tried harder to focus.

"Okay, so what does all that have to do with me?"

"Your aunt hired us to spy on Bode," Sabrina said. "Now that she's gone, we don't know who to report to."

"We don't feel our services are needed any longer," Seton said, "given the new relationship between you and the Jenkinses."

"Ah," Rafe said, the light beginning to dawn. "Because Julie's pregnant, you feel a conflict of interest."

"Yes." Seton nodded. "There's a baby to consider. We can't spy on the grandfather of the child you're expecting."

Rafe blinked. "So all the information you were giving my aunt on Bode's comings and goings…"

"Is now terminated." Seton stood. "It's not right for us to live there and spy for you when there's a baby who might be harmed by something we report."

"Well," Rafe said, "I see your point. You realize Bode is a bad man, and my aunt hiring you, while perhaps sneaky, was a very clever plan."

"But we have to think about the baby," Sabrina pointed out, "so you're on your own."

Rafe sighed. "Did you ever tell my aunt anything pertinent?"

"Practically his every move, though I don't know how it was all that useful. I think Fiona just liked knowing she was putting one over on Bode," Seton said. "But Julie's become one of my dearest friends."

"Very unprofessional of you, but understandable." Rafe liked Julie, too. It would be easy to like her, even if he didn't lust for her as he did.

"Clown," Seton retorted. "I'm being professional by telling you that there's a conflict of interest."

Rafe nodded. "Sorry. You're right. Okay, from now on, we Callahans are on our own. We always have been, you know, so it's no big deal. Your services have been greatly appreciated." He cleared his throat, trying to look like a man who knew how to think his way out of a box, as his aunt had bragged. "So, does this mean you are moving out and living with Bode and Julie? Because obviously Sabrina can't live here and you, Seton, live there. Who knows who could trust whom?"

The sisters looked uncomfortable for a moment.

"We're hoping you'll trust us to remain living as we are," Sabrina admitted. "I like living here. Seton likes living at Bode's."

"He's a crusty old man, but I don't mind him." Seton shrugged.

"Hardly private investigator work," Rafe observed. "More like caretaker and cook." He looked at Sabrina. "Why are you still living with us? Fiona had you helping with correspondence and her duties. She's not here any longer." Rafe was truly curious. "I guess if you two aren't going to be moles any longer, then you have no reason to live at Rancho Diablo, Sabrina."

He was just musing out loud, thinking about this new gnarl in the Callahan affairs and how Jonas would feel if Sabrina decided to depart, so he was surprised when Seton said, "I told you he'd say that," to her sister.

"It's okay," Sabrina replied quickly. "He's right. I'll go."

Rafe sat up, realizing he might have just stepped in a big one. Jonas had a thing for the little gypsy faker. Jonas had never said as much, but it didn't take a man of huge IQ to see that Rafe's oldest brother seemed to lose a little focus when she was nearby. In fact, Jonas hadn't taken a woman out since he'd come back to the ranch, Rafe realized with some alarm. "There's no rush, of course. My aunt would—"

"I'll be staying with my sister," Sabrina said. "If your aunt ever returns, I'll be happy to come back to work for her."

Seton got up from the leather chair. "I feel much better

now that we've talked. Thanks for listening to us, Rafe. We were starting to feel caught in the middle."

Sabrina nodded. "It's so important to have a clear conscience. I'll move my things out from the main house. And, Rafe, thanks for everything."

He blinked, watching the sisters leave the barn. "Oh, this is great," he muttered. "Jonas is going to kill me. And I don't think Sam's going to be too happy, either."

So much for getting out of boxes.

TWO HOURS LATER, RAFE WAS clearly the bad guy in the Bait and Tackle. He could barely enjoy the delicious burger placed in front of him, since his two brothers appeared ready to cram it up his nose. His fine aquiline nose. Rafe sighed, hating being the bad guy lately. It seemed he was wearing the black hat quite often now.

"You did what?" Jonas demanded. "Who gave you the right to do anything without a family council?"

Sam's face wore outrage in its normally easygoing creases. "I'm the lawyer in the family. I get a vote on what's legal, right and proper when it comes to all things Callahan. How dare you kick out those beautiful women?"

"To be fair, Seton didn't live here," Rafe pointed out.

"But she was here every day because her sister lived here, goose," Sam said. "And now we're just a trio of unhappy bachelors with nothing in the fridge and no hot chicks upstairs."

"You had no right." Jonas frowned, his black brows drawing level with each other. "What made you think you were the head of the household?"

Rafe held up a hand. "I didn't know they'd been spying for Fiona. They indicated that they'd become uncomfortable with the situation now that Julie's having a baby—"

"Which is your goof-up, not ours," Sam said. "It shouldn't

cost us women on the premises just because you can't read the directions on a box of condoms."

"Holy cow," Rafe said. "They wanted to go!"

"Because you weren't quick enough to figure out how to invite them to live with us, instead of Bode." Jonas shook his head. "You go over there and get them back."

"They won't come." Rafe stared miserably at his plate. "Seton is still employed by Bode and Julie. Julie will need more help now that she's expecting a baby. Sabrina didn't want to live with us because she had no real employment now that Fiona's gone."

"We need our adventurous aunt back." Jonas pushed his plate away and drank his beer.

"I couldn't agree more," Rafe said.

"What we need are jobs for ladies." Sam looked as if a lightbulb had parked over his head.

"Sabrina isn't going to be our cook," Rafe said morosely. "She has a real career. She doesn't want to take care of us."

Jonas drummed his fingers on the table. "Trust you to go and mess up everything that was working just fine."

"Yeah," Sam said. "If you'd just marry the woman, everybody could settle down again. We told you to marry her, but no, you had to go cost us ladies. Now when will we see them? Think Bode's going to let us in on Saturday nights? I think not." He slugged down more beer. "Get that judge to the altar, Rafe, for the love of Mike."

Rafe's jaw dropped. The music in the bar was loud, but didn't drown out the rushing in his ears. "I can't do that."

"Why not?" Jonas demanded. "It's what big boys do when their pants don't stay zipped."

"She hates me," Rafe said. It tore him up to have to say it. "She nailed her bedroom windows shut, she hates me so much."

Sam shook his head. "Just because you've made a bumpy bed doesn't mean we all should have to lie in it."

Rafe threw his napkin on the table along with some money. "Not to be an ass, but you guys were barking up the wrong trees with Sabrina and Seton, anyway."

He stalked out of the bar, not feeling good about his bitter words, but tired of being the bad guy. His brothers didn't understand.

He'd marry Julie in a heartbeat—even though she'd rather cut out his heart than have him.

Chapter Six

On the fifteenth of October, Rafe couldn't take it another day. He showed up on Julie's doorstep with roses, knowing very well he wasn't going to get past Bode.

He didn't. In fact, he didn't get past Seton and Sabrina, who stared out at him and his pink roses as if he were some kind of interplanetary being.

"Julie doesn't want to see you," Seton said.

"Come on, ladies. I need to see her." He gave them his most winning smile.

In the background, he heard Bode roar, "Who the hell is bothering me?"

"He doesn't like visitors," Sabrina said. "You know that."

"I don't particularly care what Bode likes. I need to see Julie." Rafe frowned at Sabrina. "And you need to come back home."

Long blond hair waved as she shook her head. "Rancho Diablo isn't my home, Rafe."

"You lived there for over a year," he pointed out. "It's more your home than this is."

"I've been scoping out some new journalism opportunities." She blinked at him, quite serious about her announcement. "I've got a few hot leads on some jobs, so I don't plan on being here much longer. Why wouldn't I want to be with my sister, though?"

Jonas was going to have his head if Sabrina went off and he never saw her again. Rafe saw that quick action and a silver tongue were needed. At the moment, he seemed to possess neither. He looked at Seton with a pleading expression. "Can you talk some sense into her? She belongs at the ranch with us. We have more than half a dozen toddlers running around who depend on a consistent environment."

Seton shook her head. "My sister is quite sensible." She took the flowers from his hands. "I'll give these to Julie," she said, and shut the door in his face.

He stared at the closed white door. Then he trotted around the house to stare up at Julie's window. Taking a chance, he hurled a few pebbles at the glass.

Julie's face appeared for a moment, then disappeared. Rafe waited a few minutes, then sighed and went to his truck. This was not good.

At least Bode hadn't tried to shoot him.

But Julie hadn't invited Rafe in, and that was going to have to be fixed. Soon.

"HE WENT AWAY MORE PEACEFULLY than I expected." Julie put the roses in a vase and carried them to Seton's room.

"Why are you giving those to me?" she demanded.

"Because I don't want my father to see them. I haven't told him yet about the baby. I have to choose the appropriate time."

Sabrina and Seton stared at her. Julie sighed. "It's difficult. He hasn't been feeling well. I don't want him to have a heart attack or something."

Actually, she knew full-blown war would break out once she confessed. It was so hard to bring that down on Rafe's head. But she was starting to swell, and surely it couldn't be much longer before her father noticed.

The next hearing for the court case wasn't scheduled

for another month. She had to do something between now and then.

And she couldn't avoid Rafe forever.

"Is there anything we can do?" Sabrina asked.

Julie shook her head. Sabrina had once posed as a fortune teller with the circus, but there were times when she was eerily prescient. Julie didn't want to talk about Rafe anymore in case Sabrina chimed in with something she didn't want to hear. Having lived with the Callahans, Sabrina knew them better than Julie did. "I don't think there's anything anyone can do. I'm just waiting for the right moment."

"There's no such thing as a right moment," Sabrina said cheerily. "All moments are what we make of them."

Julie sighed. "I knew you'd have some piece of advice that would make me feel guilty." She did feel a little guilty—okay, a lot guilty. Guilty about her father, and guilty about Rafe, and even about this baby, who would grow up in this weird existence between two families who couldn't stand each other. "Thanks for everything, girls," she said. "I appreciate all you're doing for my father and me."

She went out to take a walk in the late October sun, soaking up the last bits of autumn before the season began to change. Halloween would be upon them soon enough. The little girls at Rancho Diablo would be old enough to trick-or-treat now, but Fiona had never allowed trick-or-treating. She'd always given a little Halloween party, complete with a friendly scarecrow the girls could admire, and pumpkin-colored cupcakes—organic and gluten-free, of course. The girls had been so little, still babies, and Fiona didn't want anything scary around them. Her boys, Fiona said, had been afraid of everything when they were young.

Julie smiled, and then gasped when she realized Rafe was standing at the end of her field. He waved, and she decided she couldn't run off again. "Hi, Rafe."

He didn't look at her stomach, which Julie appreciated, because she felt self-conscious enough in the leggings and oversize orange top she wore.

"Hi, Julie. You look well."

She thought if anyone looked well, it was Rafe. The man was gorgeous. But it wasn't simply that; he was kind, too. She checked out his dark blue eyes and wide chest, broad shoulders and dark hair. Nerves prickled her scalp. It was just all too much to take in at once. "How's the family?"

"Fine. Growing. Busy." He shrugged. "How do you feel?"

"Never better." It was true. Thankfully, pregnancy seemed to agree with her.

"I assume you haven't told your father, since he hasn't come waving his shotgun."

Julie didn't particularly appreciate the reference and frowned to let him know it. "I'm waiting for the right moment."

"Good luck with that."

There wasn't really anything left to say, Julie decided. They were just too far apart, on everything. "I've got to go back in. What are you doing out here, anyway?"

"Checking out trenches. And these fences. One got cut, so we had to repair it." He looked at her, one brow slightly raised.

"You think my father did it."

Rafe shrugged again. "Don't know why he would."

Anger flared inside her. "Still, you're thinking that he might destroy your property—"

"Don't put words in my mouth. There are three women in that house at all times with your father. I'm not sure when he'd have a chance to get into mischief." Rafe shook his head. "My brothers raised hell on me when Sabrina left. I don't want any more trouble between the houses of Callahan and Jenkins."

"There wouldn't be trouble," Julie snapped, "if you and your brothers weren't always looking for it."

Rafe didn't say anything. His gaze was so clear, so honest, that Julie knew she'd taken offense too quickly. He was trying to be nice. "I'm sorry."

He shook his head. "No worries. Hey, I'm going to get back to work, Julie. But it was great seeing you. Let me know if you need anything. Anything at all."

His gaze jumped for a fraction of a second to her stomach, then he turned back to the four-wheeler he was driving.

"Rafe," she called.

He turned. "Yeah?"

"I am sorry."

"For what?"

She didn't know how to put it in words. "For everything. The awkwardness. The pregnancy. Just…everything."

"The pregnancy is just as much my fault," he said.

"I could have remanded you into custody for disrespect in my courtroom," Julie said, grasping at straws. Anything to try to make it easier to say what she had to. "Instead I…"

"You what?"

She shook her head. "I wanted you," she said simply.

His eyes went wide.

"I mean, you didn't hear me saying no, did you?"

Rafe shook his head.

"Well," Julie said, feeling as if it was time to be honest and face facts for everyone's sake, "it takes two to tango. I should have told you I didn't have birth control. Now you're stuck in a terrible situation, and I think…"

He waited, his hands jammed in his jeans pockets.

"I don't see how this'll ever get better," Julie admitted.

Rafe reached out and stroked one finger down her cheek. "It has to, for the baby."

Then he got in his four-wheeler and drove away.

Julie took a deep breath and wished her conscience felt clear.

It didn't.

RAFE WAS SURPRISED to see his brother Judah riding toward him as he drove the four-wheeler home. "Hey. How are the kiddoes?"

"The twins are keeping me up at night." Judah grinned, looking happy about it. "Got a minute?"

"I've got minutes," Rafe said. "Hell, I've got hours."

Judah tied his horse in front of the house and hopped in the four-wheeler. "Let's take a drive."

"Why not? Give me the coordinates, amigo."

Judah pointed to the south of Rancho Diablo. "Head that way."

Rafe did, glancing over at his brother, who was a happy man since Darla had tied him down. "Marriage seems to agree with you."

"It would agree with you, too, if you decide to try it."

Rafe sighed. "I guess you've heard the good news, then."

"Yeah, but I'm keeping my lips zipped. This doesn't need to go past the Callahan family until you tell Bode."

Rafe's jaw sagged for a moment. "Me tell Bode?"

"You think Julie's going to?"

Rafe blinked. "I don't think that's my place."

"It probably wasn't your place to knock her up, either, but you did. Apparently with typical Callahan speed. Keep going toward the canyons."

Rafe shook his head and decided maybe his brother had lost his mind just a little to baby brain. What else could explain the outlandish notion that he should beard Bode in his den and give away Julie's secret? Judah must have forgotten how recently Bode had been aiming a shotgun at his dear brother.

"Here," Judah said, and Rafe stopped the four-wheeler. "We'll walk the rest of the way."

"Far?" Rafe asked, and Judah said, "Whine much?"

Rafe sighed. "Only when everybody's having a pound-on-Rafe day."

Judah didn't reply. Rafe followed his brother, beginning to wonder what the hunt was all about. It wasn't like Judah to wander too far from Darla, and as far as Rafe knew, the foremen, Jagger Knight and Johnny Donovan, kept watch on land this far from the house.

"I thought it was time to tell you about this," Judah said, leading him under a small outcropping and into a deeply set-back cavern.

Rafe blinked in the darkness. "How'd you ever find this? We've ridden every inch of this land and I've never seen it."

"The way it's tucked back in the cliffs hides it pretty well."

As his eyes adjusted, Rafe was astonished by the size of the cave. It was big enough to fit a lot of people into, and even horses if necessary. "I've ridden past this a hundred times over the years."

"Come on back here." Judah waved a hand to draw him farther into the cave. "See this?"

Rafe eyed the shaft and basic pulley and cart. "What the hell is it? Something to do with smugglers?"

Judah shrugged. "Maybe once upon a time. I'm not sure now."

Rafe speared him with a stare. "How long have you known?"

"A few months."

"Why haven't you told anyone?" Rafe looked at symbols smeared on the wall, and a hand-loomed Native American rug on the floor nearby, almost a temple of sorts. Or a resting place. "Why are you telling *me?*"

"Fiona didn't want anyone to know." Judah looked at him. "After she left, I wondered why I was keeping a secret of something that might affect the court case."

Rafe swept his gaze around the cave. "You think this is the rumored silver mine?"

Judah picked up some silver pieces off a low flat rock. "A few months ago, there was a different pile of coins here."

"Coins?" Rafe looked at the silver. "Silver bars?"

"Someone is paying someone for something."

"And someone is hanging out on our land." Rafe glanced around. "Smugglers."

"I'm not so sure." His brother sat down on the rock. "Fiona kept a lot of secrets, bro."

"We're not going to go through that again, are we?" Rafe was impatient with the thought that their aunt was always up to her elbows in plots. *She probably was,* he thought, *but I'm not selling her out.* "Fiona had nothing but our best interests at heart. The most I'll believe is that maybe there are poor people who come through here that she was trying to help." He looked at Judah. "Don't you imagine that was the case?"

He shrugged. "I've thought about it for many moons now, and lots of scenarios come to mind."

"Why haven't you told Jonas? Or Sam, if you're worried about the case?"

"Because you're the smart one in the family," Judah said. "You're supposed to know stuff. I'm just passing the knowledge off to you."

Rafe sighed, glanced at the blue marks on the wall. "You read Navajo?"

"Is that what that is?"

"What the hell did you think it was? Martian?"

"You're the one who studied Latin, and as I recall, some

Sanskrit. Which, might I add, I thought was pretty useless at the time."

"German, Flemish and some Mandarin," Rafe murmured. "It's helpful in the military to know how to say more than 'Yes, sir!'"

"Whatever," Judah said. "So what does it say, Einstein?"

"It says," Rafe said, "that Fiona's friend Chief Running Bear uses this cave."

Judah blinked. "Really?"

"No, dummy. It's an educated guess." Rafe went over and looked at the coins, the rock, the rug, the writing on the wall. "And my highly attuned sense of discernment tells me more than one person uses this cave."

"How do you do that?" Judah demanded.

"Counting shoe marks. There's a pair of cowboy boots, a pair of ladies' boots, which is strange, and something softer, like a moccasin. Those are popular these days in the fashion mags, you know. But I would guess also with anyone who doesn't want to leave a dedicated shoe tread." He looked at Judah. "Someone else found this cave."

"Fiona told me that Johnny Donovan and his bride had found it, but Fiona swore them to secrecy. It happened last Christmas, when they were out chasing Bleu through the storm."

"How far back in the cave have you gone? How deep is this shaft?"

"Too scared to find out. Until today, I was out here by myself." Judah shrugged. "And Fiona seemed to want to keep it secret, so I didn't bother."

"Let's go back there." Rafe was really curious.

"Let's not." Judah looked at him. "Not without our brothers, candles, rope…"

Rafe peered into the darkness. "What if we've found the

silver mine? It means Bode has a bigger reason for trying to get our land."

"Again, we don't own the mineral rights," Judah reminded him.

"But Bode doesn't know," Rafe said thoughtfully.

"And Bode doesn't know you knocked up his daughter. Life's weird that way."

Rafe ignored him. "Fiona and the chief were fast buddies and met once a year."

"Or more, if they met here. I'd say they did."

"I'd guess they did, too," Rafe said. "Check this out." He lifted the flat rock and pulled a plastic bag out from underneath. Inside were several photos.

"Strange," Judah murmured. "Baby pictures."

"Yeah," Rafe said. "All the newborn Callahans' first baby pictures."

The brothers stared at each other for a long time.

"My God, she was strange, wasn't she?" Judah said.

Rafe put the photos back in the bag and inserted it under the rock. "Fiona isn't strange. She's the most wonderful guardian we could ever have had."

"And we all kept her secrets. We never questioned her. We just let her lead us around."

"Because we love her," Rafe said. "Don't get freaky because of a few baby pictures under a rock. Jeez." But even he couldn't think of a reason for his aunt to be in this cave storing pictures. "God knows what else she's probably hiding in here."

"That's it. She's using this as a satellite storage facility." Judah snapped his fingers. "Like she uses the basement."

"You mean that long gravelike scar in the basement floor?"

"Not necessarily a grave," Judah said, "but something."

"I don't think I want to know." But he had an eerie feeling about what Judah was planning to say.

"You're going to have to dig up whatever she's hiding in the basement."

"No," Rafe said, "I'm leaving sleeping whatevers alone. You want to know, you dig."

"We could just ask her."

They pondered that for a few moments.

"We could, but she's not ready to tell us," Rafe said, and Judah nodded.

"Are you going to tell the others?" Judah asked.

"I need to reflect on what all this means." He glanced around the cave. "It might be best to keep it away from Sam, since he's the legal beagle on the case. We don't want to prejudice him from being honest. Now that we suspect this is some kind of mine, he'd have to admit it in documents. And we don't know that this is a silver mine. It could just be, like you said, a storage facility."

Judah frowned. "I think you should call Fiona."

"I might." Rafe looked around one last time, eyeing the pile of silver. "Or I might just go find the chief."

Judah stared at him. "That's why we let you be the brains of the outfit."

"Why?"

"Because you're so smart sometimes you're stupid." Judah looked at his brother with admiration. "Only you would suggest hunting down a man, who probably doesn't want to talk to you, about a cave on your own land."

"They own the mineral rights, don't they?"

"True."

"So," Rafe said, "I'm sure we're going to get the yearly visit from him on Christmas Eve, just like our aunt always did, to discuss business."

Judah considered that. "How are you going to find him?"

"Like this." Rafe picked up a piece of blue clay and wrote on the flat rock. "Chief Running Bear, looking forward to seeing you on Christmas Eve. R. Callahan." He grinned at his brother. "Looks like a holiday invitation to me."

Judah followed his brother out into the late twilight. "Too bad you're not so smart about your love life, bro."

"Yeah," Rafe said. *But Julie admitted she wanted me, and that means everything is going to start going my way, eventually.*

At least he hoped so.

Chapter Seven

"Dad," Julie said, walking into Bode's study, "how are you feeling?"

He nodded at his only child. "Fine, girl. How are *you* feeling?"

Julie went to sit by her father so they could look out the windows together. Her dad loved to sit and stare at the landscape. His study happened to face the Callahan spread, which she herself could have done without viewing.

It reminded her of Rafe, and she didn't want to think about him. Even though she did all the time.

"Tomorrow's Halloween," she said, not that it mattered. They didn't celebrate the holidays, not like the Callahans did. Fiona always strung lights like mad, and had the house festooned for every holiday, even a whisper of a holiday. Some she made up, or at least Julie thought she did. Saints' birthdays, holidays in foreign countries—Fiona liked to celebrate everything.

"Are we passing out candy?" Bode asked, and Julie smiled.

"Not this year, but maybe next."

Bode sat up in his worn wingback chair and looked at her. "Oh? Will we have something to celebrate? I'm not much for kids ringing the doorbell, you know. Any kids ringing the bell around here will likely be that crop of Callahans that's sprouted up next door."

Julie sighed. "Dad, I'm having a baby."

Bode stared at her. "You're what?"

"I'm having a baby." She took a deep breath. "In May."

Bode blinked. "That can't be possible." He looked worried.

She shook her head. "I'm afraid it is, Dad." And then, because she knew what the next question would be—the normal question any parent would ask—she went ahead and answered it.

"Rafe Callahan is the father."

Bode's face turned red. He stared at her, uncomprehending, or perhaps just disbelieving. Then he shot from his chair and paced the room before coming back to stand in front of her.

"I'll *kill* him!"

She held up a hand. "No, you won't."

"I will!"

"Dad, listen." Julie tugged her father's hand, guiding him to sit back down. She was terrified she'd give him a heart attack, or worse, a stroke. "Calm down. Rafe didn't do anything to me that I didn't want." It was so painful to admit that to her father. She felt like such a traitor. But the truth was, Rafe *hadn't* done anything that she hadn't loved every moment of.

"You hate the Callahans," Bode said, his hands trembling.

"*You* hate the Callahans, Dad. *I* barely know them."

"Obviously you know them better than I thought you did! Unless—"

"No." Julie shook her head, putting an end to what she knew her father was thinking. "I was a completely willing participant with Rafe."

Her father turned his face away and sank back in his

chair. "He seduced you. He messed with your mind. It's because of the court case, because you were the judge. I know the Callahans better than you do, Julie. If it hadn't been for the lawsuit, he'd never have looked twice at you."

Her father's words cut at her like knives. "Regardless of how it came to be, I'm having a baby with Rafe Callahan. I'm going to be a mother, and I have to act like a mother. Which means I can't spend time worrying about feuds. I have to do what's best for my child."

Bode looked at her suspiciously. "What exactly does that mean?"

"It means, Dad," Julie said softly, her hand covering his, "I'm moving out."

His eyes bugged. "That snake is going to cost me my only daughter? The comfort in my old age?"

Julie shook her head. "I'll still be living in Diablo. I just won't be under your roof. You have an excellent caregiver, and frankly, Dad, you don't need me. I blinded myself into thinking that you did, but right now—"

"He needs you more?" Bode's voice was a sneer. "I would have saved you the pain if I could have. If you think that by moving out of here, that man'll start coming around, you're wrong."

Julie stood. "It doesn't matter. It's past time for me to be on my own."

Bode's eyes went wide. "You'll need help with the baby."

"Plenty of women have a baby without help." Julie crossed to the door. "I'm a judge, Dad. I think I can make proper arrangements for my baby when the time comes."

Tears began to slide down Bode's cheeks. Julie steeled herself against her father's newest ploy. It was heartfelt emotion, she knew, but she was also completely aware that her father had always played to her affection for him. "Please don't leave me, Julie. You're all I've had after your mother died."

She went back to him and kissed his cheek, giving him a hug he gratefully returned. "It'll be all right, Dad. You'll see how much you enjoy having the house to yourself after I've moved out. I'm buying a place in town, and you can visit often, too."

"Buying a place! You've already made plans?" Bode sat up, worried. "Don't you realize how that'll look once people realize that scoundrel won't marry you?"

"*I* won't marry *him*," Julie said. "And I'm not worried what people think about me."

Bode looked at her, his gaze shrewd. "Has he asked you?"

"Rafe made some noise about us being together. I wasn't paying attention. Marriage is so far from my mind I can't even bring myself to think about it."

Bode sniffed. "Good. You can do better than a Callahan."

Julie turned at the door. "Maybe I can and maybe I can't, and maybe I don't even care. But, Dad, he's the father of my child, and from this moment forward, I don't want to hear one negative thing about Rafe. Or any of the Callahans. Can you understand my feelings?"

Her father shrugged. "Not really. Pitiful genes for the baby, I'd say." He frowned. "This isn't going to change my mind about getting their land. You don't remember what it was like when they first came here, Julie. It was quiet out here, peaceful. Suddenly the Callahans came, and a bunch of brats, and everybody liked them, wanted to be their friend. Suddenly you couldn't go anywhere without hearing Callahan this, Callahan that. And then those damn Callahans went and died, and left the brats here. I thought the county would have to be called. Your mother wouldn't hear of that, though. She was always going over there helping Fiona. Worked herself to the bone, in my opinion. And why?" Bode shook his head. "No reason at all, to my mind."

"Dad, Fiona was new to this country. I'm sure there was a lot she needed help with."

"If your mother had stayed home with me, where she belonged, she'd probably still be here. The Callahans destroy everything they touch."

"Dad," Julie said softly, "I'm so sorry for what you've gone through. But surely you know it wasn't the Callahans' fault."

He closed his eyes. "I know what I know. Go. I need to nap."

Her father's skin was pale. He looked lifeless in his chair, his hands dangling over the sides. Julie's heart broke, knowing how much she'd hurt him. "I love you, Dad."

He didn't say anything. Tears jumped into her eyes. She left his study and went to find Seton.

"Can you check on him in a little bit? He's had a bit of a surprise." Julie picked up her keys and her purse. "I've got a doctor's appointment, so I'll be out for a while."

Seton looked at her, her blue eyes wide. She set down the bread she'd been kneading, and wiped off her hands. "You told him, didn't you?"

Julie nodded.

"Was he very upset?" Seton handed her a glass of water she didn't want. Julie took a sip, surprised by how dry her mouth was.

"It wasn't the happiest day of his life."

"Not even to know he's going to be a grandfather?" Seton was incredulous.

"No," Julie said, her voice breaking a little. "He never said anything about the baby."

"He'll come around," Seton said, but she didn't sound certain. Julie nodded, put the glass down and left.

There wasn't any reason to think that Bode would ever forgive the Callahans.

Or her, for that matter.

JULIE WASN'T COMFORTED to see Rafe waiting by her truck. It was unfortunate that he made her heart pound and her breath catch in her chest. After the discussion with her father, she had the strangest urge to throw herself into Rafe's arms and have a small meltdown.

She was a Jenkins. She didn't do meltdowns.

"Now's not a good time," she told Rafe, who shrugged.

"Probably never going to be a good time," he replied. "I get that you don't want me sneaking in to see you. That leaves me hanging around, hoping you'll make a run to the grocery store. You look great, by the way."

Julie slung her handbag into the truck. "Thanks. You don't look so bad yourself, which I'm sure you know."

Snarky. She was being rude and snarky, and Rafe had no idea why she was all wound up. "Look, I'm not having the best day," she confessed. "So I'm not up for small talk."

"That's all right." He gave her the winning smile that never failed to make her heart flip over—when it wasn't making her mad. "I'll buy you a hamburger."

"No." She got in her truck. "I don't want you to buy me anything."

He leaned against her window so she couldn't shut it. Too near, too much chest, too much handsome male staring in at her. Julie felt hot, even though it was late October.

"We need to talk." Rafe shrugged. "Sooner rather than later."

He was right. Julie sighed. "I'm really busy these days."

"Tell me about it. Bribing Seton to give me your schedule today was not easy. She says you're always going ninety to nothing." He frowned. "I hope that's not unhealthy for you."

"Don't concern yourself with my health," Julie snapped. "You should be more worried about yours. I just told my father that he's expecting a grandchild. Let's just say he's not a happy person right now."

"Hot damn," Rafe said, his tone awestruck. "It's a wonder he's not out here with a shotgun."

"He doesn't know you're here." Julie put the keys into the ignition, a trickle of unease sliding through her. "If he did, there would be all kinds of uproar. I'd appreciate it if you wouldn't deliberately antagonize my father, Rafe. He has health issues."

She frowned when Rafe laughed out loud. "Sorry, sweetie. There's nothing wrong with that old man except that he's mean and stubborn as hell. He's kept you tied to him like a nanny all your life so he won't be lonely." Rafe leaned in and brushed her lips gently with his. "Don't worry about me, lamb chop. I'm not afraid of your old man, who is arguably the worst shot in the county."

Julie sucked in a breath. "You're contemptible."

"Ah, but we're not in court, are we? It's just me and you, sugar." He went around the front of the truck, which Julie thought was brave of him—or arrogant, since she could pleasantly run him over right now. When he got in the passenger side and grinned at her, she wished she had the desire to throw him out.

She didn't.

"You can't go with me. Get out," she said, but her voice sounded unconvincing even to her. "I'm going to the gynecologist, and no man wants to go there."

"I do." Rafe perked up. "It'll be good for me to be around other pregnant females."

Julie shook her head. "There is always a pregnant female at your ranch."

"But I don't pay attention to them. Their moods are not

my concern." He tweaked a lock of Julie's hair. "Your moods are much more interesting. Right now, you seem all bothered to me. The way you marched out to the truck made me think that all's not well in the house of Jenkins. Now you tell me your father knows about the baby, and therefore his new relationship to me, and I wonder to myself, has that got my little judge's robe in a twist?"

She frowned at his question. "You sound so happy about it, but no, I'm not in a mood because of my father."

She was, but family was family. Rafe was the enemy. He didn't need to know anything about her father. "I'm not happy that you're in my truck," she said. "Can you blame me? You're nothing but trouble."

"You have been talking to your father. You know, doll," Rafe said, leaning back and pushing his hat down over his eyes, "for the sake of the baby, you're going to have quit letting your father fill your head with fantastically evil fairy tales about the other side of the family. You might even start thinking of us as the good guys."

"I don't think so," Julie said, feeling snippy. "I'll drop you off in town. If you even darken the door of my doctor's office, I'll tell them to call the sheriff."

"Sheriff Cartwright thinks highly of me." Rafe sounded unconcerned, and possibly sleepy. "He'd be amazed that you'd made such a catch, Julie Jenkins."

She rolled her eyes, started the truck and rumbled down the drive. "I wouldn't catch you if you were a catch, Rafe Callahan. My father says you're all a bunch of thieves."

Rafe chuckled under his hat. It annoyed her, and she was in no mood to be more annoyed than she was.

On the other hand, she wondered if maybe once Rafe saw the baby on the monitor, he might realize this was a real person, a child, something that was going to change his life forever.

Maybe he'd leave her alone.

"You know," she said, her tone casual, "maybe you should come in while I'm at the doctor's."

He ripped the hat off his face. "You mean, to the appointment?"

"I'm having a sonogram. We'll probably be able to see something that looks like a baby by now. Most of the time, the sonogram just looks like black-and-white lines and holes to me." She beamed at him. "I don't know for certain, but maybe you could hear the heartbeat, too."

Rafe seemed relieved. "That would be cool." He gave her a careful look, then sat back. "Why'd you change your mind?"

"Can't a girl do that?"

He snorted. "Yeah. All the time. In your case, Judge, no. Never. Not without reason."

"Oh," Julie said airily, "suspicious Callahan."

"Suspicious Jenkins."

They left it at that.

Twenty minutes later, Julie wanted to scream.

In fact, she did let out a hysterical squeal of denial. "That's not possible!"

The doctor looked more closely, as did a nurse and a technician. "Definitely triplets. See? There's one, two, three…"

Rafe was sitting as close to the screen and her as he possibly could. "That doesn't sound right. My twin, Creed, had only one baby with his wife. Multiples don't always run in our family. Pete's the only one fortunate enough to have three, but he's the responsible brother."

The doctor looked at Rafe as if he were daft—or in denial—and he figured he was. He swallowed hard. "I don't see three babies."

"I don't, either." For once they agreed. Julie was afraid she was going to hyperventilate.

"Absolutely certain on this one," the doctor said, and the technician nodded. "It's too soon to tell the genders, and we might have difficulty doing that, anyway. Depends on how they situate themselves in the—"

"Stop." Julie sat up, wiped the lotion off her stomach. "I'll come back another day. I had a hamburger, and maybe that—"

"Calm down, love. We haven't eaten yet." Rafe pushed her down on the table with a gentle hand, and Julie surprised herself by lying back. "Take a deep breath. Think of this as the happiest day of your life."

The medical personnel in the room were studiously trying to listen, but the endearment and the concern Rafe was showering her with had them somewhat agog. At first, perhaps they'd assumed she'd brought Rafe along for moral support. Maybe as a birthing coach. Although that would have been stretching it, considering the long-standing lawsuit that everyone in town had been following for years.

But now...now everyone would know Rafe was the father.

Julie jumped off the table. "I'm getting dressed. Rafe, you wait out in the waiting room. Better yet, don't wait at all." She forced back tears.

Everyone cleared out of the room with sympathetic glances.

"She'll calm down in a bit," Julie heard the doctor say to Rafe once the door closed. "Often mothers get a bit emotional upon seeing their firstborn in utero. And multiples are always a shocker."

Julie pressed her hand to her stomach. Three babies! The Callahan curse! She flung the door open to find Rafe standing on the other side.

"I thought I'd wait to see if you needed anything—"

She pulled him inside the room. "If I didn't know better, I'd say you made triplets on purpose!"

"No." He shook his head, but his deep blue eyes twinkled. "If I could train my sperm that well, love, I'd have gone for four. I need four to take over the ranch. My brothers are ahead of me. Pete, you might recall, has trips. I definitely would have gone for the big win."

She smacked him on the chest.

Rafe grunted and rubbed at his pectorals, which she knew were rock-hard, amazing and wonderful.

"That's dumb," Julie said. "None of you are going to have a ranch to take over."

He pulled her into his arms. "Now, Judge, this is not the time to be all competitive. You just won the grand prize. Go ahead and cry, gorgeous. You deserve a weep."

She started to push off his nicely warm, comforting chest, and then thought *maybe this once I will be a little silly and cry.*

"Judges don't cry," she said, and he handed her a tissue.

"Did your daddy tell you that?" Rafe rubbed her back, comforting her.

"No, but he always said boys didn't, and neither should I."

"Julie Jenkins, it's time for you to quit letting Daddy run your life."

"I know," she said, with a last sniffle. "And he's going to be so sad."

"Nah, he's tough. He'll get over it. And it'll be good for him." Rafe held her away from him, stared down into her face. "You ever stop to think that if you give the old man some independence, he might find a woman and settle down? And then the whole county could relax?"

"That's awful." Julie let Rafe crush her back against his chest. She thought she could hide there for a few more minutes. What could it hurt? No one saw her being emotional. "Know any ladies his age?"

Rafe laughed. "Let's go get that hamburger. You're eating for four now."

"Don't remind me."

Yet Julie went with Rafe, trying to decide if maybe he wasn't as bad as she'd always thought he was.

He probably was. But it was time to find out.

Chapter Eight

A week later, Rafe was still overwhelmed. He had too much on his plate to brag. He wanted to boast like mad, but figured it was Julie's right to put the word about, let everyone know that the Callahans had struck again.

He hadn't even told his brothers.

"It's almost miraculous," he muttered to Bleu, as he tossed hay into the feed box. "Except for Creed, who's a bit slow anyway, we've all gone multiple."

Bleu snorted, the equivalent of an equine shrug.

"You don't care now, but wait until there's three little boys tugging at your mane, wanting a ride."

Bleu looked as if he was certain he wouldn't put up with those kinds of shenanigans. Rafe laughed and went on down the wide aisle, checking the horses they'd put in the barn. As Novembers went, it wasn't that cold yet. Soon enough it would be. He liked knowing the horses were snug in the barns at night.

He'd like knowing that Julie was safe and snug in his room at night.

Ever since his lady had found out he'd knocked her up in a trophy-winning way, she'd been a little uncommunicative.

"I'm just about ready to deliver myself to Julie in a giant tub of chocolate ice cream," he told Bleu, coming back to gaze at Rancho Diablo's favorite horse.

"Hello?"

Rafe turned to look in the direction of the female voice. "Hi," he said, shocked to see Julie standing in his barn. "Long time no see."

Her brows rose. "A week?"

He cast a quick glance at her tummy, which was rounding nicely with his offspring. "You look great."

"I look plump. I think it's subconscious. As soon as I heard 'triplets,' I started eating a lot more."

Rafe nodded. "I'd eat more, except I'm responsible for the grub around here now. One thing I've noticed is that if I cook it, I don't want to eat it. At least not much of it."

She hesitated. "I want to show you something."

He wanted to see anything she wanted to show him. "Let me wash up."

Rafe made fast work of that, then joined Julie as she led him to her truck. "Taking a drive, are we?"

"We are."

There were a thousand questions he wanted to ask. Had she told Bode—or anyone? Rafe didn't have a pound of lead in him, so he figured Julie had been as silent as he had. Seton and Sabrina never came around anymore, so he wasn't certain what was going on at Chez Jenkins.

"You know," Rafe said, deciding other subjects were safest, "my brothers are none too happy that Seton and Sabrina moved to your house."

"Oh, don't worry." Julie turned down a drive in town. "Sabrina's not with us anymore."

He blinked. "Where is she?"

"She took a job up north, I think." Julie's brow furrowed. "Wait, I remember. She's in Washington, D.C."

Jonas was going to be furious. "Doing what?"

"She got a job. I'm not certain what she's doing. Seton says her sister writes for newspapers."

Ha. If Julie knew that Sabrina had been a plant to spy on Bode, she'd flip. For that matter, Seton was also a plant, and a more serious one, because she wasn't just an investigative journalist hired by Fiona, she was actually a private investigator.

Not that she'd been worth beans, Rafe thought. She was more loyal to Julie these days. "Does Seton ever date anyone?" he asked, making his tone casual.

"Why would you want to know that?" Julie sent a glance his way that he felt despite the approaching evening hours.

"I don't know. Just wondered. Not sure why a young, beautiful girl like that would want to coop herself up with an old man."

"It may shock you, Rafe Callahan, but not everyone thinks my father is running the evil empire."

Rafe held up a placating hand. "Hey, let's not go over that again. I'm all for getting along with the in-laws and the out-laws."

Julie stopped in front of a small, two-story white house in a cul-de-sac one street off the main town drag. "Here we are."

"Where?" he asked, getting out, since Julie was.

"Home sweet home." She beamed, then put a hand on her stomach without realizing she did it, which Rafe thought was cute and very mamalike of her. "This is my new house."

Rafe turned to look at the small place surrounded by a few split-level adobes. "Someone didn't care for the tried-and-true Southwestern style?"

"I guess not. It's all right, though. It has everything I require. Come on in." She pulled out a key and unlocked the door.

Rafe followed her inside. "It's been redone. That's nice."

She nodded. "It has so much of what I need for raising three children."

He turned to her, wanting to tread carefully. "You didn't want to live with Bode anymore?"

"Weren't you the one who said I needed to let him do his own thing?" Julie shrugged. "It was time for me to have my own place."

He nodded. "Julie, I—"

The words wouldn't come to him. He wasn't certain how to express what he wanted to say. Congratulations were in order, he could see that. Any man knew that when a woman purchased her first digs, she was standing on her own two feet. A house purchase was a serious thing.

But didn't they need to live together as a family?

Quite obviously, that thought had never occurred to Julie.

"It's nice, Julie," he said, as she waved him into the kitchen. "Real nice."

"I've already gone grocery shopping to fill up the cabinets." Julie smiled, pleased, and continued the tour. "Laundry room with a sink off the kitchen. I figure the extra sink will be handy." She was like a girl, showing him all the treasures of her new house. "Four bedrooms upstairs, and an office down. Or I could switch it, and have a master down and an office up. While the babies are small, we're all going to sleep upstairs."

He swallowed hard, barely able to think. "This is great."

"You really think so?"

He wasn't about to deny the delight in her voice. It was a huge step for her to get away from her father. "I do," Rafe said with conviction. "Congratulations. This house ought to be a wonderful home for you and the boys."

She looked at him, one slim brow rising. "Boys?"

"The babies."

"They're girls, Rafe."

Silence fell in the kitchen.

"All of them?" he finally asked, and Julie laughed.

"I don't know. The doctor can't tell yet. It's too early to know."

"So they could be boys," Rafe said.

Julie grabbed some cookies from the cupboard and put them on a plate. "You sound like my father. He was always disappointed I wasn't a boy."

"No, he wasn't," Rafe said, following her as she went upstairs. "I have it on good authority from Fiona that you were the apple of your daddy's eye."

"Yes, but he would have preferred a boy. And I don't want you doing that to our girls."

"Not me," Rafe said, noticing that the "master" bedroom was about the same size as a tack room at Rancho Diablo, and not a very large one at that. He'd be lucky if he and Julie both had enough closet space in here. "Hey, girls are great. I'm all about girls. If we're having girls, I say break out the pink."

Julie laughed. "My girls will wear blue. And whatever other color they like."

"Works for me," Rafe said swiftly. "Break out the blue."

She looked around the room, ignoring his noble attempt to be easygoing. "The movers come tomorrow."

"Need some help? You don't want to overdo things."

"No," Julie said, "I've got Seton and some friends helping me."

"Friends?" An unbidden, unwanted spark of jealousy shot through Rafe. "Like, guys?"

"Yes," Julie said. "All your brothers, if you must know."

His jaw sagged. "I thought you said *friends.*"

She came to stand in front of him. "I'm trying, Rafe. I have no desire to let the past stand between my kids and their family. So I invited your brothers."

"What about me?"

"I need some space from the men in my life. I hope you can understand that."

"I don't know," Rafe began.

"I brought you here tonight, didn't I? You're the first person who's seen my house, except Seton."

"Well," Rafe said, slightly mollified, "I'm still very good with carrying and unpacking boxes."

"Thank you," Julie said, "but no."

"All right," Rafe said. "But I'm not used to being left out."

She laughed and went down the stairs. He followed, watching her sweet derriere sway, while automatically cataloging all the changes that needed to be made to the house to make it baby-safe.

Baby gate at the top of the staircase. Plug covers to keep little fingers out. Et cetera, et cetera.

He figured she probably wouldn't appreciate him interjecting his opinions. Maybe if he kept his mouth shut, Julie would invite him back.

Basically, he needed to prove to her that he wasn't going to over-own her like Bode had. It wasn't going to be easy to achieve some distance, when all his senses were screaming to possess her.

But he had to give her space. Otherwise, he was never going to get her into a real bed.

And that would be a shame.

RAFE SAT OUTSIDE ADMIRING the night sky, and thinking how much a full moon agreed with Julie, who was in full nesting mode, when a shadow at his elbow made him sit up.

"You wanted to see me?" a male voice asked, and Rafe jumped to his feet.

"See who?" He peered into the darkness and saw nothing but an outline.

The figure came closer. In the light from the house windows, he recognized the chief.

"Why would you think I want to see you?"

"Got your message." Chief Running Bear grinned. "No point in waiting until December twenty-fourth, is there?"

"Any time is good with me."

"What can I do for you?" the older man asked.

Rafe narrowed his eyes. "Why did you meet my aunt every year? What's going on in the basement?"

The chief shrugged. He wore jeans, a flannel shirt, boots and a hat, looking much like anyone else in the town. "That's between me and your aunt."

"My aunt is gone."

His companion nodded. "I know."

"So I need to know what she was working on down there."

The chief gave him a long look. "If she'd wanted you to know, she would have told you."

"Not necessarily. Fiona kept a lot of secrets."

The chief shrugged again. "What else?"

Clearly, the man wasn't going to talk about Fiona. Rafe sighed. "Does your tribe own Rancho Diablo's mineral rights?"

He inclined his head. "It was our land before we sold it to your parents."

Rafe thought about that for a moment. "You know Bode Jenkins has filed all kinds of suits to get our land taken from us."

The chief shrugged again. "It won't happen. This land is yours. As part Native Americans, you are entitled to this ranch."

Rafe shook his head. "We're full Irish. Our parents were straight off the boat. So were our aunt and uncle."

"Your mother, Molly, was Irish, your father, Jeremiah, full

Navajo." The chief looked at Rafe. "The land will always be your family's. This is Diablo land. Shall we walk?"

Rafe figured the chief didn't want to be seen by anyone. He fell into step with his visitor, wondering why Fiona had never told them of their true heritage. "So this whole plot of my aunt's to give the ranch to the person with the most children was just an excuse to get us married."

"Once the lawsuit happened, we knew that the land had to be safeguarded. The only way to do that was to split it up among you. Extracting anything from six brothers, their wives and children, and their estates, would be a difficult thing. Your aunt did want you settled down, but you would have all gotten your portions in due time, anyway."

Rafe shook his head. "Such a complicated way to do business."

"I liked her idea. Family is a good thing."

"Maybe." Rafe thought about Julie and how he was ever going to get her to agree to become one big happy family with him. "So you own the mineral rights, which Bode doesn't know, and so he can't get those. We have the land in our possession, and he can't get that. Shouldn't we just tell him?"

"No," the chief said. "He believes everything can be solved if he just greases the right palm with silver."

"Speaking of silver," Rafe said, "is that a real silver mine?"

The chief nodded. "It is. It's not a working mine anymore. It could be, but it's so small it would only be worth mining silver for jewelry. What was most valuable was dug out long ago."

Rafe nodded. "So why are you hanging out in the cave now?"

"Storage. It's an excellent storage facility." His broad face creased with wrinkles and a smile. "No one would ever find anything in there."

"Fiona used it."

The chief nodded. "It's safe."

Rafe wondered how safe. He'd seen many footprints in the cave. "We found photos of all the Callahan babies. What was that about?"

His question earned him a shrewd look from the chief. "That you must ask your aunt."

Rafe grunted. "I intend to. I'm planning to head over to Ireland to see my cagey aunt and tell her there wasn't any reason for her to leave. She didn't have to go, and she knew it. And I know it now."

"She felt like the family was better off without her. She'd served you well."

"We're better off *with* her." Rafe was certain about that. "Unless she doesn't want to live in New Mexico."

Impenetrable brown eyes met his. "It was home."

"She shouldn't have left."

"Fiona did not want Mr. Jenkins focusing on her any longer. He can't get over the fact that he believes his wife died because she was taking care of Fiona and your family too much. Mrs. Jenkins was ill, though. She wanted to do what she did for Fiona. Mr. Jenkins doesn't like to accept the things he knows to be true. He's angry."

"You're telling me," Rafe said, but he felt a twinge of sadness for the bitter old man.

"He's not going to like you for taking his only child away from him," the chief pointed out. "Have you considered that your children will likely not have a willing grandfather?"

Rafe squinted at him. "How do you know about my children?"

"I knew long before I heard it in town." The tall, still-vital elderly man smiled. "You know, your parents wanted one thing—a large family."

Rafe stopped walking to stare at him.

"I knew your parents," Chief Running Bear said, "and I know their children, and I will know their grandchildren." He nodded. "This has been a good talk. We'll talk again one day."

"Wait," Rafe said, but then realized the chief was walking away, not listening anymore. Rafe had a thousand questions to ask, more about his family, his parents, his heritage. But just then a sharp whistle rent the air, and a black Diablo mustang ran toward the chief, who launched himself at a dead run onto the horse's back. "Holy smokes," Rafe said, "I thought I was a good rider."

He watched until man and horse disappeared into the night, and then he turned toward home, wondering if he was any closer to knowing what he had to know.

RAFE WALKED INTO THE upstairs library, surprised to find Jonas and Sam there already, toasting each other in front of a small fire. They had a couple snifters of brandy, which was a bigger surprise, because typically they relaxed with a beer. "Family meeting been called that I should know about?" Rafe asked.

"We're celebrating." Jonas swirled his snifter. "Come in and join us in the festivities."

Rafe wasn't feeling all that celebratory after his chat with Chief Running Bear. While he'd been digging up the family ghosts, his brothers had been indulging themselves. But he took the snifter Sam handed him, and sat down near the fire. He felt cold, chilled.

It was all the talk of the past that had him feeling as if he was stuck in a meat locker.

"So what are we celebrating? The full moon? A new

lady?" Rafe gulped some brandy, knowing he was putting off the inevitable. He was going to have to tell his brothers what he'd learned—and it was going to change them as much as it had changed him.

"Lots." Sam grinned. "First, your hot judge has got herself some new digs."

"Don't I know it." Rafe set the brandy down, deciding he needed a clear head.

"It's a start, getting her away from Bode. You're smarter than you look, bro." Jonas grinned.

"I had nothing to do with it."

"You had everything to do with it," Sam said. "You got her pregnant, and that alone deserves some kind of trophy. I didn't think anyone would ever get Julie away from Daddy."

"Don't make it sound like she's some kind of silly girl whose father makes all the decisions for her." Rafe felt cranky hearing his woman discussed in such a cavalier manner. "Anyway, what else are we toasting?"

"Jonas finally put in an offer on the Dark Diablo Ranch." Sam's face was gleeful. "Combined, we'll have fifteen thousand acres."

Rafe's jaw sagged. "Why?"

Jonas shrugged. "If I've learned one thing from Bode, it's that land is power. With land, you're safe. You have a place to call your own. And, basically, I was tired of putting up with him. We'll just move ranch operations over there if he bugs us too much, and put a monster hotel right here to drive him nuts. Maybe a high school. Something with lots of lights and noise to keep the old geezer up at night."

Rafe blinked. "Do you think we might have discussed this?"

"It's my money," Jonas said. "All you boys go on and have babies by the truckload. I'm happy to be King Jonas. Everything I touch turns to land."

Rafe glanced at Sam, who shrugged. "What's gotten up your nose, Jonas?" Rafe pressed.

Their oldest brother leaned back in his chair, savoring his brandy. "All the years of Bode yapping at us. I just want to be free. I want more of what matters most."

He was really going to freak when he learned that Sabrina had moved to Washington, D.C. Rafe took another swig of brandy, coughing as it went down the wrong way.

"Easy," Sam said, "it's brandy, not water. Meant to be rolled across the tongue, not slung down your hatch."

Rafe sighed. "Here's the thing. While you two have been sitting up here in your ivory tower feeling good about life, I've been down on the ground taking in the lay of the land."

"Here comes Mr. Sunshine. Brace yourself," Jonas said, pouring Sam some more brandy.

Rafe took that comment in without a word. "First, the gossip. Sabrina's picked up stakes and gone to Washington, D.C."

Jonas stared at him. "What the hell are you talking about? She would never leave her sister."

"She did." Rafe nodded. "She got a job, and that was that."

"Washington, D.C.?" Jonas asked, his tone incredulous. Rafe felt sorry for him.

"Yes. That's the gossip." Knowing that he'd poleaxed Jonas for the moment, he went on. "And I just had the most interesting discussion with our friend Chief Running Bear."

"What?" Sam sat up. "How did that happen?"

Rafe didn't mention that he'd left a message in the cave for Fiona's friend. "It just happened. Just now, as I was standing outside."

Jonas glowered at him, still not happy about the Sabrina bulletin. "And?"

Rafe shrugged. "He doesn't say much. I got the feeling he's keeping a lot of Fiona's secrets. However, he did mention that we're not full Irish, like we thought we were. We're half Navajo, courtesy of our father. Fiona is our mother's sister, but we were always told she was our father's sister."

Sam and Jonas stared at him, taking in the ramifications of his announcement.

"I suppose," Rafe said, "it would explain why we all have blue eyes and black hair."

"That doesn't make sense," Sam said. "Fiona said she came from Ireland to take care of us because she was our father's sister. Fiona is completely Irish. Therefore, our father couldn't have been Native American."

"Did she say it, or is that how we remember it?" Rafe thought about this angle for a moment. "Where are our aunts and uncles, grandparents? Any relatives?"

"Why didn't you ask the chief?" Jonas demanded.

"I was in such shock I didn't get everything out I wanted to know. And frankly, we could ask questions for twenty-four hours, and we wouldn't know everything." Rafe gulped some more brandy, welcoming the fire as it burned down his throat. "I was more focused on Rancho Diablo and the Bode issue."

"You realize I'm the only one here who probably isn't related to the rest of you. God only knows where Fiona got me," Sam said.

"From under a rock," Jonas said, not cheery now that he'd learned Sabrina had left. "Finish the story," he said to Rafe.

"Chief Running Bear said Fiona left to protect us. He said that the land will always be ours. His tribe does own the mineral rights. Bode can never really get our land away from us, considering that the mineral rights and the land are split. And I suppose, with the tribe being involved, the government won't take any land away from them. I mean, obviously." Rafe shrugged. "So we're home free on that issue, since we may be part Navajo."

"Bode doesn't know any of this," Sam said.

"No." Rafe nodded. "And now that you know, you'll have to declare it."

"I need to see documents first," Sam said. "Easy enough to look up land ownership and mineral rights through court records."

Rafe nodded again. "We wouldn't need the Dark Diablo property, Jonas. Unless you want it."

His brother shook his head and didn't reply.

Sam walked over to the fireplace. "And it wasn't necessary for Fiona to leave—"

"Except she was afraid Bode was so mad at her he might hurt one of us," Rafe reminded him.

"But it's dumb," Sam went on, "that we don't just tell Bode to stick it in his ear—"

"Easy," Rafe said. "I'm trying to marry his daughter."

His brothers stared at him. "You are?" Jonas demanded.

"I thought Julie wouldn't have anything to do with you," Sam said.

"She's having my babies," Rafe said. "She's going to have to get with the program sooner or later."

"Babies?" Sam exclaimed.

"Triplets," Rafe said, practically boasting. "Let it never be said that the Callahan men don't shoot straight as an arrow."

Jonas shook his head. "Disgusting. Meantime, you and your blabbermouth ran off Sabrina."

"I didn't do it," Rafe said defensively. "Sabrina wanted a real job. She wasn't working for Fiona anymore. You're going to have to deal with the fact that your little gypsy wasn't really a fortune teller, Jonas. She's a career woman who couldn't sit around here waiting for you to decide to get off your sawhorse and ask her out."

Jonas blinked. "This isn't Six Brides for Six Brothers, as

much as Fiona might have wanted it to be, Rafe, and as happily as you're falling in with The Plan."

"At least Seton's still around." Sam sipped his brandy. "Maybe that means Sabrina will be home for Christmas, Jonas. Anyway," he said, raising his glass to Rafe, "congratulations, bro. Excellent shooting. They say the smart ones have little to no common sense, and I guess you proved the theorem."

Rafe wasn't sure what Sam was driving at. Sam wasn't a mathematician, he was a damn fine lawyer. And if Rafe knew one thing about math, it was that a theorem proved was a theorem true. He wasn't certain, but he thought Sam had just claimed that he'd done something dumb by getting Julie pregnant. Then again, what the hell did Sam know about geometry and math in general? Or even women?

He looked at his brothers, realizing how stuck they were. Neither one would go after the lady he wanted. They'd sit here all day, claiming they weren't interested. Locked in their towers, as usual. *I'm not stuck, though. I've got my woman. And she knows exactly how I feel about her.*

Well, maybe not exactly.

After Julie moved into her new house tomorrow, maybe Rafe would tell her.

Chapter Nine

"Where've you been?" Bode demanded of Julie as she returned home from showing her new house to Rafe. She was all wrapped up in dreams and thoughts of the future. It shouldn't have mattered, but she'd been proud to show her place to Rafe. She wanted him to see where his children would be raised. That was fair, wasn't it?

Despite the past, she meant for him to be a welcome part of his children's lives.

"I told you, Dad. I went by my new house."

He shook his head, agitated. "You didn't tell me."

Julie turned to look at her father more closely. His tone was more querulous than usual. "I didn't tell you, specifically. I asked Seton to tell you."

Bode frowned. "Seton's not here."

"She's not?" Julie stared at her dad, wondering how long he'd been alone. "Do you know where she is?"

"I don't know. She said she was giving notice." Bode's frown grew deeper. "She said she was moving to Washington to be with Sabrina."

Julie's mouth dropped open. "Dad! Why didn't you call me on my cell?"

"Would it have made a difference? You're leaving, too." Bode sat back, a stubborn, unhappy lump in his chair.

"I…" Julie glanced at her father. "I'm not leaving. I'm moving fifteen minutes away."

"Same as leaving." Bode looked out the window. "Anyway, she just up and left. I guess you'll be doing that tomorrow."

"You can come to the new house and help me unpack boxes." Julie refused to allow her father to dim her happiness. "You know, Dad, you don't really want to live in a house with a bunch of children. You think it wouldn't be that bad, but you're used to peace and quiet."

Bode stiffened. "Children? As in future children?"

"No," Julie said, keeping her voice calm, "children as in I'm having triplets."

A red wash flooded Bode's face. He bounded from his chair, leaping to his feet so fast and hard that he knocked over the end table. "Damn those Callahans! Nothing but trouble, every last one of them!"

"Dad!" Julie frowned at him. "Calm down!"

Her father's head swung around. "How can I calm down, knowing that those Callahans, those damn Callahans, who've taken everything I have in life, have stolen my daughter?"

"Hardly stolen." Julie shook her head. "You need to stop looking at the Callahans as competition. They're not. As far as I can tell, they're barely aware that we're over here."

A sharp bark of laughter escaped Bode. "Aware enough to put a bull's-eye on my daughter!"

Julie crossed her arms. "I'd appreciate it if you never say another cross or unkind word about the father of my children. I mean it, Dad. Please."

He frowned, sweeping her with a disbelieving gaze. "What's happened to you? What's made you change? It's like a spell's been cast on you."

Julie's expression matched her father's. "What do you mean?"

"It means," Bode said, his tone furious and betrayed, "that once upon a time, you knew what it meant to honor your father. Now all you do is talk about that Callahan like he's some kind of prince."

"There are no princes and no villains. I'm simply accepting my life as it is." Julie gave her father a pleading smile. "Dad, let's not fight. We're going to have three beautiful babies. That should put back a whole lot of what you feel has been stolen from you."

"See? See?" Bode wheeled his arms. "*What I feel has been stolen from me?* Like I'm making the whole thing up." Bode stared at her, disbelieving.

"There are two sides to every story. I've been a judge long enough to know that." Julie turned to leave his study.

"You used to know which was the right side," Bode said, his tone filled with bitterness. "Before you got your head turned."

"I have a lot to do. If you want to come to the house tomorrow, you're very welcome. If not, it's your choice."

Julie left her father, not feeling good about it, but not knowing how to fix it, either. He simply didn't realize she just couldn't go on living in the past.

His past.

"Not my past," Julie whispered, putting a hand to her stomach for just a moment to feel the babies there, "and certainly not yours."

She could only think of her children's futures.

THE NEXT DAY, JULIE was aware of Rafe hanging back, watching his brothers unload everything. Her father had elected not to come, and if he couldn't be pleasant, then it was for the best.

The other man in her life, who also seemed unhappy, clearly wanted to be a participant in the move. Julie fought off the guilt, telling herself that both men were going to have to learn that not everything could go their way all the time.

"Don't mind him," Sam said, walking by with a flowered ottoman. "Rafe's a suffering succotash if there ever was one."

"He's so pitiful," Julie said. "Maybe I should—"

"Nope." Sam jerked his head toward the house. "Show me where this flowery thing goes."

She followed him into the house, and pointed to the den. "Right there, please."

Sam grinned. "It'll serve Rafe right to have to put his feet on this." He looked at the huge, tufted pink-yellow-and-blue ottoman with glee. "Rafe deserves every bit of this girlie stuff."

Julie blinked. "You don't think he'll like it?"

Sam chuckled. "He'll feel right at home."

Julie didn't think Sam was being quite honest. Maybe the things she'd bought were a little on the feminine side, but did it matter? It was her home, her first home.

"Your dad decide not to come?" Sam asked, heading back out for more items.

The other brothers kept up a steady stream, carrying things from the van they'd rented, and the Callahan women and some of Julie's friends unpacked, refusing to allow her to lift so much as a cup.

"My father is at home, upset that his little girl grew up." Julie smiled when Sam glanced back at her. "He's also in a bit of a mood because Seton left."

Sam gave her a sharp glance. "What do you mean, left?"

"Just left. No notice, no nothing. No goodbye." Julie was still annoyed—and hurt—about that. She'd considered Seton a true friend.

"I don't believe it," Sam said. He thought about it, then shook his head. "Nope. She wouldn't do that."

A tiny trickle of unease flowed over Julie. "Well, she did."

Sam pulled a pie table from the truck. "Now here is piece of furniture just made for a man to sit a beer on."

"Stop." She put a hand out to impede Sam's progress. "First of all, I'm aware that you're having a giggle at my expense. You think my stuff is too feminine for Rafe. It doesn't matter. Your brother doesn't live here, and isn't going to be moving in," Julie said, her tone stern.

"Yes, ma'am," Sam said, having the decency to look a little respectful.

"Rafe never implied he'd want to live here, and I'm looking forward to life on my own."

"Yes'm." Sam gazed at her, his blue eyes twinkling.

"Second, what do you think happened to Seton?"

"Me? I'm just a lawyer. How would I know?"

Julie gave him a look that spoke volumes about his innocence ploy. "Counselor, I'm not in the mood for word games. I'm a pregnant lady with mood swings. Let's respect that."

"Yes, ma'am!" Sam grinned hugely.

"So what do you think happened to Seton?"

The smile slipped from his face. "My guess? Your father's throwing a hissy fit because you moved out. He fired Seton and told her to go without saying goodbye to you." Sam shrugged. "That's my guess, based on years of watching Bode get what he wants."

Julie's face burned with anger. "Put the table down," she said, her tone soft but sharp, "and go."

"Julie—"

"Go," she said, and turned away.

She heard the pie table being set gently on the ground, heard boots walking away. She was so mad she was shaking. Of course, she'd asked him, practically forced him to tell her what he thought.

Yet she hadn't expected Sam to have such a vile opinion of her father.

And if Sam had that kind of totally wrong take on him, likely all the Callahans felt the same way. Including Rafe.

What had she expected?

She glanced down the street, seeing Rafe leaning against his truck. Sam had gone straight to his brother, no doubt filling him in on her "mood swing."

But what Sam had accused her father of was so dark, so manipulative, that she could barely imagine him thinking it. Her dad would never have dismissed Seton—fired her—just to try to make Julie regret moving out, to try one last thing to keep her tied to him.

He wouldn't have done it.

Julie went back inside to unpack.

BY NIGHTFALL, AFTER everyone had left, Rafe decided the time had to be right to take Julie a housewarming gift—namely, himself. He rang the doorbell, holding the set of rubber-tipped cooking spoons he'd bought her, arranged nicely in a clay pot of beautiful Native American design. He was pretty proud of himself for shopping for something practical, when he'd really wanted to buy her a see-through nightie.

Spoons first, then nighties, he told himself. *Play it cool.*

Julie opened the door and stared out, not exactly smiling at the sight of him.

"Hello, Julie," Rafe said. He extended the pot. "Brought you a housewarming gift."

She glanced at the spoons. "This isn't a good time."

He didn't know what to say to that.

Julie decided to jump into deep water. "I'm sure you know about the conversation Sam and I had."

Rafe looked at her, thinking she was beautiful even when clearly annoyed. Being attracted to your woman even when she was mad was a good thing; if a man could stand his woman in a mood, their relationship was sure to be a go. "He didn't mention anything to me. Sam's the baby of the family. He teases a lot, but he's harmless."

She shook her head. Rafe thought she looked tired, which was reasonable, given her long day, but it also alarmed him. Her blue dress stretched over her stomach, which, he noted, was filling out nicely to accommodate his boys. "You look hot, Julie. Sexy hot. Drive-me-crazy hot."

She gave him a wry look. "That line shouldn't work, but I'm afraid it does. Come in, you silver-tongued devil."

"I'm serious," Rafe said, slipping in the door before she could change her mind. "You can't let Sam get to you. He doesn't mean anything he says."

"He does when he's in court."

"Yeah." Rafe removed his hat and tossed it on a flowered mushroom-type footstool near the sofa. "But when he's not in barrister mode, we barely pay attention to him. Trust me, he's like your favorite farting grandfather. You just don't know what he's going to say or do, so you just ignore it and hope everyone else does, too."

He could see that Julie was trying not to smile. "This is serious, Rafe."

"All right." He seated himself next to the hat on the floral tuffet, even though he wasn't certain if men were supposed to sit on such things. Maybe they were meant only for ladies, hence the puffs and fringe and ribbons. "Tell me what's on your mind. But can you come a little closer while you unload? If this Venus flytrap swallows me, I'll need you to pull me back out."

"What is it with this ottoman?" Julie didn't step closer. "Sam had the same reaction."

Rafe patted the sides. "It's like a pregnant cupcake. Didn't Jeannie have something like this in her bottle?" He bounced a little, testing it. "Not like my leather sofa at home, which is substantial and manly."

Julie laughed. "It does look a little like something out of *I Dream of Jeannie.* Get off. I'm sending it back tomorrow."

"No, you're not. I like it. I really do." Rafe didn't like it at all, but he didn't want to hurt Julie's feelings. If his pumpkin liked it, then he'd learn to love it. "You realize my boys are going to use this as a launch pad."

"My girls will sit on it and look pretty," Julie retorted.

Rafe shrugged. "So, Judge, what did Sam do to get himself kicked out?"

Julie took her attention from the ottoman, putting it back on him, where he liked it. He sat up, enjoying having her dark eyes looking into his. "I told him that Seton had left my father's employment unexpectedly, without even a goodbye to me."

Julie put her hands on her hips, which he watched with interest. His buttercup was spreading out in that area, developing a goddess body. Rafe got an erection just thinking about how her curves were blossoming. "Doesn't sound like Seton."

"Exactly. And Sam's theory is that my father fired her."

Rafe's gaze left Julie's hips unwillingly and settled on her face, which wasn't exactly a hardship. She was so beautiful, he thought. He couldn't wait to kiss her mouth again—he never got to kiss her long enough to suit him. "Did you ask your father if that's true?"

"No. I didn't think that far. Sam's reasoning is that Dad did it so I'd be guilted into staying in his house."

Rafe blinked, thinking it was entirely plausible the old man had done exactly that, but realizing this was a moment for great diplomacy. Boot-scooting around the facts, as it were. "Sam talks a lot. He's a lawyer." Rafe shrugged. "What does that have to do with you being mad at me right now?"

"I'm pretty sure you feel the same way about my father," Julie said.

"Ah…" Rafe hesitated. "It doesn't matter what I think. Sam cares what happened to Seton because I think he's got a thing for her. I'm just trying to stay out of trouble with you, Judge."

Her lips pursed. "My father wouldn't have fired Seton. He liked her a lot."

Rafe put up his hands. "Don't ask me. Ask your dad what happened to her. In the meantime, give me something to unpack. I don't want you lifting a finger, gorgeous."

Julie stared at him. "Rafe, this isn't going to work."

He put on his best innocent face. "What isn't?"

"Your family, my family. In-laws and out-laws."

"I don't care if it does. I care about you, and my children, and that's all I have to care about." He got off the stuffed, frilly footstool and went to her, enveloping her in his arms, even though he worried he might be moving too fast for her. "I don't care what Sam or your father says. I don't care where Seton is, or anybody else, at the moment. All I care about is you."

Julie gazed up at him. "That might be a good idea."

"That's right. You listen to me, and everything will be fine."

She put her head on his chest, which he liked very much. He held her close, enjoying her being a little more relaxed than usual.

"You know, you have a tendency to talk a little like a male chauvinist at times," Julie said.

He chuckled. "I'm certain the best judge in the county can keep me in my place."

"You remember that."

Rafe wondered if it was too soon to try to sneak a kiss. He decided it was. "So, friends?"

She looked up at him. "Until you annoy me."

"Sounds like marriage to me," Rafe said, and kissed her on her forehead. "Give me something to unpack."

"You can put your spoons in the kitchen." Julie handed him the pot he'd given her. "Why spoons?"

Rafe took his gift into the kitchen. "I sure wasn't bringing you a knife set, sweetie."

"You're smart," Julie said, and Rafe smiled.

"That's what they tell me, Your Honor. That's what they tell me."

WHEN RAFE FINALLY ENDED up in a bed with Julie, it didn't happen the way he thought it would.

"No," he said, steering her away from unpacking in her room, "you're not doing a thing. You sit on that bed and see how well I take direction."

"I don't want you unpacking my personal things," Julie protested. "That would feel so strange."

"Tough." He held up a blue nightgown. "This is pretty."

"Closet," Julie said with a sigh.

Rafe dutifully trooped into the closet and hung it. Returning to the box, he pulled out a sheer white nightie. "I like this one better."

"It's going to be a slow process if you inspect all my undergarments," she said.

"I'm not in a hurry." Rafe handed her some nighties. "As intriguing as unpacking Victoria's Secret is, you handle this stuff, and I'll go do the dishes and pots. I don't want you lifting heavy things."

"You won't know how I want my kitchen set up. And I'm very particular about my kitchen."

Rafe ran his finger down Julie's nose. "You're particular

about your nighties, too. Some might say you have a bossy streak, Julie Jenkins."

"They would not. I'm particular, which is different from bossy."

Rafe smiled. "I like a woman with opinions."

"I don't care what you like," Julie retorted.

"I tell you what I don't like," Rafe said, glancing toward the stairwell, "I don't like that staircase. It scares me. You're getting quite, um, stately. What if you fell? What if one of my babies falls?"

Julie looked at him. "My father's house was a two-story. Your house has several stories."

"Three," he said absently.

"And more than one staircase."

"Front, back and secret." He shrugged. "This one's steep. I don't like it."

Julie's dark brows rose. "Rafe, it has a handrail."

"Yeah." He scratched at his stubble, wondering why his little darling hadn't had the common sense to purchase an adobe one-story. The thought of little feet trying to negotiate that bear of a staircase bothered him. "All right, I'm going down to do the kitchen. You do your bedroom. I figure if we get these two rooms more settled, you're good to go until the ladies come back tomorrow to help."

"They were mostly interested in setting up the nursery. And they unpacked the living room, laundry room, craft room, all those things that take hours. But the nursery got the most attention."

Rafe's head whipped around from the box he'd been perusing. "I didn't see a nursery."

Julie waved a hand. "Open that door across the hall."

He walked to the door with a giant Pooh bear stuck on it. "I would have preferred a cowboy or a football player, but Pooh it is," he muttered, and opened the door.

He was shocked to see three white cribs set up with mobiles hanging over them. A white rocker sat in a corner, and a giant woven circle rug graced the wooden floor. "Wow. This is something else."

Julie came to stand beside him. "Makes it real, doesn't it?"

"Yeah." His heart was banging around inside his chest. "Scary real."

"That's the first time I've heard you admit you're scared."

"Spitless, at the moment." Rafe turned to look at her. "When are these babies due?"

"May." Julie smiled. "It's not even Thanksgiving. We have a while to adjust."

Rafe thought he was having his first panic attack. "Let's let you lie down for a moment," he told Julie. "You look a little pale."

"*I* look pale?" Julie stared up at him. "You look pale, Rafe. Like you've seen a ghost jumping around in your—"

"You definitely need to lie down." He stumbled toward Julie's bed, collapsing on it as manfully as he could. "You'll feel better in a moment, I'm certain. And I'll get you a cold drink of water, which will help."

She put a hand on his brow. He liked the way her skin felt cool and calming against his. His pulse was going faster than he'd ever felt it. "Funny how this dizzy spell just all of a sudden came over you, isn't it?" he asked.

"It sure is." Julie sank down next to him, running her hand over his face. "One of us feels kind of clammy."

"Yeah," Rafe said, "although I've never understood what clammy means. What is clammy? Have you ever thought about what a strange word that is? I could understand it if people said sweaty, or 'your skin is moist.' But what is clammy, anyway? Where did that come from?"

"Dear heaven," he heard Julie murmur, "I actually let you get me pregnant."

Rafe waved an expansive hand in the air. "That was easy. Callahan sperm can swim through a maze to find the perfect egg."

Rafe thought she said something about someone being an overly arrogant ass, but he wasn't certain. Her bed was so soft, and Julie felt so clammy—whatever that meant, but she'd said it, so it had to mean something—that he thought the best thing for her to do was rest. He decided to join her in a small nap until she started feeling better.

I have to look out for her. She's such a delicate little tulip. I'll protect her from everything.

Chapter Ten

"Then he fell asleep." Julie looked at the two tall, strong, handsome men sitting at her kitchen table the next morning, gazing at her with sympathetic, dark-denim eyes just like Rafe's. "Or fainted."

"Did anyone ever mention that Rafe is the odd one of us?" Sam asked, seeming almost pleased that his brother had a weak spot. "He faints when he sees blood, particularly his own. I'm pretty sure baby poop and spit-up are going to be way beyond his powers to stay upright."

Julie nodded. "That just may be true. However, I'm still annoyed with you, so tell me again why you're here?"

Sam glanced at Jonas. "To apologize. I shouldn't have said what I did."

Julie placed a cup of coffee in front of each of them. "You shouldn't think it, either."

"That's true." Jonas gave Sam a warning glare as he sipped his coffee. "Julie's part of our family now. Since Rafe can't take care of her, we'll have to look out for her. In the future, guard your tongue."

Sam appeared chastened.

"Now, look," Julie said, sitting back down. "I don't need anyone taking care of me. Your brother needs more help than I do. Frankly, I'm just focused on trying to get along with my children's family."

"Despite the lawsuit." Sam nodded. "We're all for that. We're all about the joys of being uncles."

"The lawsuit has nothing to do with me," Julie said coolly. "I'm not the judge hearing it, so I don't care."

"And you've got your hands full with your pregnancy," Jonas said, his tone kind. "I'm sorry our brother went lights-out on you. He's an excellent pilot, but he may not be that great a birth coach."

"I haven't asked him to be a birth coach." Julie frowned. "I wouldn't want Rafe anywhere around me while I'm giving birth."

"Oh," Sam said, "that'll kill him."

She thought about the big cowboy still flung across her sheets. Rafe had fallen like a giant oak across the width of the queen-size bed. The bed had protested the weight falling on it, and Julie had been relieved when it didn't collapse. She'd briefly considered pulling off Rafe's boots, then decided not to. He had to be uncomfortable, and yet he seemed perfectly happy.

She'd left him there, listening to him snore while she unpacked more clothes. After about twenty minutes, she'd decided she needed a nap, too, and had crawled up alongside him. He'd immediately snuggled into her back, cupping her stomach with his big hand.

Truthfully, she'd enjoyed the intimacy.

"So, what brought you here so early in the morning, anyway?" Julie asked, telling herself that thinking about Rafe was unproductive. It would take a forklift to get him out of her bed, and so it was best to let him sleep off whatever had hit him.

"We saw the lights on, and Rafe's truck, and decided to make sure our brother wasn't annoying you." Jonas smiled. "Since he wasn't supposed to be here yesterday."

Julie nodded. "I might have been a bit hard on him. But this house means a lot to me, and I want it to feel completely my own."

"Understandable," Sam said jovially. "We wouldn't want him, either."

"True," Jonas said, "except he's a decent cook, so we let him come around."

She knew they were teasing her. Still, it was difficult understanding the byplay of brothers, since she'd been an only child. And she wasn't used to such a large family. It had surprised her when the doorbell had rung at nine o'clock in the morning.

Then it came to her: the Callahans were treating her like part of their family. Despite the lawsuit, despite her father, and no matter what happened between her and Rafe, they were going to include her.

Julie liked the feeling of security that knowledge gave her. "Does he always sleep like a dead man?"

Jonas nodded and got to his feet. "We all do. We can drag him off with us, if you like."

She considered that. "That's all right," she said. "I'll kick him out when he wakes up."

Sam got up, too. "Thanks for the joe. And let us know if you change your mind about Rafe. We're used to dragging one or the other of us out of strange places."

She smiled as they went out her door. "Thanks for checking on me."

They tipped their hats and departed.

Julie glanced around the living room of her new house. After a moment, she went back upstairs and looked at the man engulfing her bed.

Then she got back in with him. His arm instantly covered her, tugging her close.

It was the best thing she'd ever felt.

"No, no, no," Rafe said an hour later as he sprang off the bed. "Didn't I tell you? If you feed them, they keep coming around. You'll never get rid of them."

Julie smiled as he stretched and tried to work a kink out of his back. "I had to feed your brothers. They said you weren't there to do it."

"Helpless. I have to do everything for them."

Julie nodded. "I know."

He threw her a suspicious glance as he rubbed his stubble. "Are you feeling better?"

"Wonderful. You?"

"That bed may be smaller than I like, but it's comfy." Rafe patted it. "However, I think I pulled a muscle in my back."

"Unpacking nightgowns is tough work." Julie got up from the bed. "I'm kicking you out now."

"That's okay. I need to go supervise the Rancho Diablo affairs, or nothing will be done right. In the meantime, you go downstairs, sit on that flower thing and rest."

"I'll do that," Julie said, and Rafe glared at her.

"I'm serious. Moving is hard work."

"I know. It nearly killed you." Julie patted his shoulder. "Be careful of the staircase. That might kill you, too."

"You laugh," Rafe said, his boots clomping as he walked down the stairs, "but phobias have always been good to me."

Julie giggled. "I'm sure."

"Well, remember, there's your chair." He pointed at the flowered ottoman. "I don't want to see you anywhere but on that when I return with your dinner. You're having organic salad, fruit, and a steak to put good red blood cells in my boys."

"That's not quite the way it works. And you don't have to bring me anything," Julie said, ignoring his confident insistence that he was having males, unlike his brothers.

Rafe stuffed his hat down on his head. "I have to look out for you."

"I've taken care of myself for nearly thirty years."

"And look what happened the first time a real man looked at you." Rafe brushed Julie's hand across his lips. "You let him seduce you in a field."

She withered him with a stare. "That's all right. I'm keeping him at arm's length now."

"Yes." Rafe ran a gentle palm down her cheek. "That's got to change."

Julie closed the door after he went down the steps. She leaned against it for just a moment, her eyes closing. Rafe was a lot of man to "keep at arm's length."

Did she want to anymore?

JULIE KNEW SHE COULDN'T put off visiting her father any longer. So at lunch, she swung by Banger's, grabbed her father a burger and went by to see how he was doing.

It was almost as if he knew she was coming. He sat in the darkness of his study, his face arranged woefully.

"Turn on some lights," Julie said, flipping on a few lamps. She handed him the hamburger bag. He set it on the table beside him while she sat on a chair nearby.

"You're going to have to get over all this, Dad."

He looked at her. "My only daughter running to my greatest enemy. How do you expect me to get over it?"

"I don't know, but you'll have to." Julie frowned. "I know it's hard, Dad, but I've got children to think of. I can't live in the past."

"The past." Bode snorted. "It's not the past. It's the right now. It's the future."

"It can't be for me."

Her father looked at her. "You probably want me to drop the lawsuit."

Julie sighed. "It's not my business what you do. Rafe and I have never discussed it, anyway."

"It's why he got you pregnant."

She shook her head. "That's not what happened."

"You can't deny the coincidence of it. The man never asked you out before, and suddenly, you're having his children. It makes me look like an old man who got bested in court and in my own home." He shook his head. "Never in all my years did I think you'd be my weak link."

"I'm sorry you feel that way."

Her father looked at her in a way he never had. "I don't think you are. I think he's turned your head. I believe you honestly think he'll ask you to marry him."

Julie glanced out the window, seeing the afternoon sun beaming despite November's early herald of winter. "I don't think of marrying Rafe."

"Well, that's something. Pregnant but not married. Your mother must be turning in her grave."

Julie got up. "Dad, I'll be back later in the week. If you want to see my new house, come anytime."

Bode shook his head. "There was no need for you to buy a house. I'm sure he told you that you needed to get away from me. Driving in those spikes, the way the Callahans always do."

"Perhaps you've misjudged them."

"Maybe you don't know them like I do."

"It doesn't matter now." Julie picked up her purse and walked to the study door. "I love my new house, Dad. Maybe you wouldn't be so afraid if you saw that I'm not that far away."

"That's not what I'm afraid of." Bode looked at her. "I'm afraid that you've been the victim of the Callahan plots. They're great pranksters, you know. Always looking for the setup."

Her father was going to be destroyed by bitterness, but there was nothing she could do if that was the path he chose. "Dad," Julie said suddenly, "did you fire Seton?"

He stared at her, his white brows beetled over his eyes. "Who says I did?"

"No one. I just wondered," Julie said. There was no reason to bring Sam's wild guess into it.

Her father shrugged. "Yeah. I fired her."

Julie held in a gasp. She stared at him. "Why?"

"Because she was a private investigator."

"No, she wasn't. She was a home care provider."

Bode laughed. "That was the story."

A chill passed over Julie. "What story?"

"The one the Callahans gave her to feed us. So you hired her." Bode smirked. "She was a plant, courtesy of Fiona."

Ice jumped into Julie's veins. "That can't be true."

Bode shrugged. "Papers are on the desk."

"You had her investigated?" Julie stared at the papers with some horror.

"Anyone who's hiring a home health care provider has them checked out. She's a private investigator, and her sister is an investigative reporter. They were hired by Fiona to dig up dirt on me."

Julie felt all the blood rush from her face. She'd thought Seton was a friend! She'd trusted her!

She'd trusted Rafe. And begun to trust the Callahans.

"The lawsuit," she murmured. "It was all about the lawsuit."

"It really wasn't that hard to figure out," Bode said. "They're Corinne Abernathy's nieces. And Corinne, of course, is one of Fiona Callahan's best friends. So in the end, Fiona tried to pull a fast one on me, but once again I was too smart for her."

Julie felt ill. "Oh, no," she murmured, thinking how Rafe

must have laughed at her. The whole time she'd been falling in love with him, he'd been plotting against her. He'd known about his aunt's devious mission to best Bode. They'd influenced Julie to recuse herself. She'd gotten pregnant by Rafe. She'd fallen for him—so easily.

Chapter Eleven

Rafe balanced a picnic basket and a bottle of nonalcoholic champagne as he rang Julie's doorbell around six that evening. The champagne to celebrate her new home and independence—and the picnic basket because he was dying to see her again. What lady could resist the charm of a red-and-white-checked picnic basket?

He had delicacies in the basket a master chef would appreciate, all for his lovely judge.

Julie opened the door wearing a scowl, which did not bode well for him. Rafe went into charming mode.

"Dinner is served, madam. Steak grilled to perfection, baby peas, French bread, mushrooms sautéed in—"

"I'll be dining alone. Thank you." Julie took the basket from him. "I won't need the bubbly."

She started to close the door.

"Hey!" Rafe saw his picnic basket disappearing and held the door open. "Julie, what the heck?"

"The heck is that you're a snake."

"Oh. Are we back to that?" He inched the door open a little more—gingerly, so she wouldn't notice—in order to gain a better look at his turtledove. She didn't disappoint, as usual. A teal-colored dress slid nicely over her breasts and hugged her tummy, which was getting quite bodacious, if he did say so himself. "You're too pretty to hold a grudge."

"You're still a snake. Let me shut the door."

Rafe sighed. "Have you been talking to your father?"

She gave him a long stare. Rafe felt his romantic evening slipping away.

"I don't have to talk to anyone to know that you're a member of the serpent clan."

"Oh. You *have* been talking to your father." Rafe shook his head. "What lies did he tell you this time?"

"No lies. Just facts." Julie frowned. "I'm fully capable of making my own judgments."

"I know." Rafe nodded. "Don't I at least deserve a trial?"

"All right." Julie set the picnic basket down on her dining room table and returned to the doorway, fixing him with a distinct glower. "Your aunt hired Seton and Sabrina McKinley to spy on my family."

Rafe nodded. "You know, I think you have that right."

She put a hand on a shapely hip. "You think?"

"Well, it's not like Fiona keeps us informed about all her doings. I do recall her saying something to that effect, but it was several months ago. And I don't think they ever told her much. I couldn't swear to that, because I don't know." He shrugged. "Anyway, after Fiona left, they decided all their loyalties had to be with your family, since that's where Seton was employed. So Sabrina moved out."

"Your aunt is exactly what my father always said she was. Trouble," Julie stated.

"Oh, come on, everyone loves Fiona. Anyway, she was only protecting us."

"From what?" Julie demanded. "My poor old father?"

That got Rafe's attention. "Julie, let's not paint Daddy with a romantic brush. He's no saint."

"Well, he doesn't plant spies!"

"Sure he does. More stuff has gone missing around our property than we can keep up with. Not to mention how many times he's shown up at a family function with a firearm. Which, I might add, you never even bothered to call the law about, Judge."

She sucked in a breath. "Rafe Callahan, you're as bad as your aunt."

The conversation was not going his way. Any hope he'd had of getting back into that cozy bed upstairs with Julie was just about obliterated. War was being declared here, and Rafe decided that if he was going to be branded a rat, he might as well go out rat-style. "What was Fiona supposed to do? Let your father steal our property for no reason? Bode has no right to it, none. He's been a crook and a cheat for so many years, he's forgotten how to play a straight hand. And you've looked the other way, Judge. You've enabled him. Which I can't really understand, because you're such an independent woman. But all this daddy-knows-best crap's hurt a lot of people even more than us."

Julie burst into tears.

"Julie—" Rafe began, only to eat his words from the force of the door slamming in his face.

"Damn," he said, "so much for getting along with the in-laws and the out-laws. Damn, damn, damn."

Romantic dinner shot, he got in his truck and drove to town to nurse a beer in Banger's.

And try to figure out how he was going to fix the problem with the judge. She didn't trust him at all.

He really couldn't blame her.

"I COULD HAVE TOLD YOU not to mess with a pregnant woman." Sam waved a longneck at him and grinned. "And let's not forget your *turtledove* has a bit of the temper in her."

"Yeah." Rafe stared at his beer. "But I shouldn't have laid it on quite as thick as I did."

"True," Jonas said, "but better to have these little pourparlers in the beginning of the relationship rather than later. Clears the air."

"Whatever," Rafe said. "She acts like her father is some kind of white knight or something. Saint Bode. I was trying so hard to be restrained. I didn't bring up all the evils her father has committed over the years. I didn't ask her what made him decide one day that he had to have what was ours. No, I stuck to the facts. Merely, that he's a weasel."

Sam laughed. "Good money says you don't ever get a foot back in her house."

"Better money says he never gets her to the altar," Jonas said, his tone morose. "The first Callahan not to get his woman wed. Hope you're not setting a trend. We wouldn't want our reputation sullied in this town."

Rafe grunted. "Appreciate the rich sympathy from you two. Anyway, Julie going on about Fiona made me lose my customary cool. If you put Fiona and Bode side by side, everybody knows who'd be voted Sly Dog of the Year."

"It only matters how Julie sees it," Jonas says, "because she's carrying your progeny. Therefore, you have to dance to her tune."

"Apparently I don't have a proper ear for tunes," Rafe said.

"Or know how to dance," Sam added agreeably. "The judge is going to sue you for all kinds of custody, probably. The Jenkins are a litigious bunch, you know."

He did know. "Bode's determined to hang on."

"Yep," Jonas said, "but I would think that for someone who's supposed to have an Einsteinian IQ, you'd play your cards a little better."

"You'd think so," Rafe said, getting up and tossing some money on the table, "but unfortunately, not so much. I want to show you something."

"We don't want to go to Julie's," Sam said. "We don't

want her mad at us. I barely wormed back into her good graces. As an uncle, it's important to be on her good side. I don't want your bad rep rubbing off on me."

Rafe grimaced. "For a lawyer, you sure do have a fear of confrontation. Come on."

JONAS AND SAM STARED AT the cave Rafe took them to, clearly as surprised as he'd been by its existence.

"How could we never have seen this?" Jonas asked. "As kids we spent our time looking for nooks and crannies in the canyon."

Rafe shook his head. "You'd have to be positioned just right to see it. The placement in the canyon obscures it."

"But it's been found before." Sam walked over to look at the blue clay writing on the wall.

"I would guess this is Running Bear's home away from home." Rafe looked around, still amazed by the size of the cave. "It can't really be called a cave. It's sort of a mine shaft."

"A mine for what?" Jonas asked, going to inspect a rudimentary cart. "This has been here a long time."

"This is the legendary silver mine." Rafe nodded at his brothers' surprise. "Yes, there really was one on our property all along. It isn't in service, and we don't own it, but it's here."

"Wow," Sam said, going to stare down the shaft. "Probably lucky we didn't find this when we were kids. We'd likely have fallen down it."

"Probably." Rafe shrugged. "The chief says he and Fiona use this place as storage now."

"Storage?" Jonas looked at him. "For what?"

"Papers. Documents. Things they wouldn't want a thief to find. Presumably whatever they discuss every year, which I would assume pertains to the mineral rights agreements and the land." Rafe looked at Jonas. "If you get serious about buying that spread you're going to call Dark Diablo, be sure to lock in the mineral rights."

"Already done when I made the offer." Jonas sat on the flat rock and looked around. "What's the sign say?"

"I forgot to ask him." Rafe had been too surprised to ask about a lot of things. "I've called this council to share a couple of thoughts that have been on my mind." He raised a hand at Jonas, who'd started to speak. "I know. You're going to say that we can't have a council without the others. But it's the three of us who are still living at Rancho Diablo, so I want to share my thoughts with you first."

Sam and Jonas glanced at each other, then shrugged. Rafe continued. "One of us has to go see Fiona and Burke. It's time they come home. The winds of change have already blown up all over Rancho Diablo, and whether or not Fiona's here to egg Bode on doesn't matter. He hasn't calmed down in her absence."

"Well, hell. No, he hasn't." Jonas laughed. "You knocked up his daughter and she moved out. He found out his caregivers were spies planted by our aunt. What's the old man got to be zen about?"

"Still," Rafe said, "nothing would have changed if Fiona had been here. All this would have happened."

"True," Sam said. "You'd best go, Rafe. You can fly the plane and sweet-talk the stubborn aunt."

Rafe pondered that for a moment. "I'm not going. I've got a pregnant woman to romance."

"We'll settle that later. Anything else on your pea brain?" Jonas asked.

"Yeah. Now that I've shown you this, there's something we have to do." Rafe stood and turned off the flashlight.

"No ghost stories," Sam said. "Remember, Jonas scares easily."

"No ghost stories to be told yet," Rafe said. "We're going to go digging for one."

Twenty minutes later, after a fast four-wheel drive ride home, Rafe led his brothers to the basement. He stood over the long scar in the ground that had fascinated them as kids.

"I'm not digging that up," Sam said. His face looked pale in the dim light.

Jonas took a step back from where they'd always imagined a coffin had been buried. "I'm not touching it."

"What a bunch of wienies." Rafe sighed. "One of you babies ought to raise his hand to throw the first spade."

"Nope." Sam shook his head. "Nothing good lies hidden under a house, bro. Mainly family skeletons and things you don't want to bring up from the ground. I say we all go upstairs to the library and have a shot of whiskey. I need it."

There were too many secrets long buried at Rancho Diablo. "Come on. What's the worst it could be?"

"What do you really want to know about Fiona, Rafe?" Jonas demanded. "What we dig up can't ever be reburied. Is that a price we want to pay?"

"You act like she buried bodies down here." Rafe wasn't going to admit to feeling a chill running down his own spine. "We *have* to know."

Jonas handed him the shovel. "So dig."

"Something's here." Still, Rafe was reluctant to find what their aunt had hidden. "We should have made her tell us long ago."

"As if she would have," Sam said.

"She might've, if we'd asked." Jonas nudged Rafe. "Want me to mark an X so you can get started?"

"No." Rafe took a deep breath. "If spirits strike me, tell Julie she was the only woman I ever loved."

"Yeah, right. She'll believe that," Sam said.

"Christmas is going to arrive before you break ground."

Jonas nudged him again. "If you don't want to do it, Rafe, let's hire someone."

Sam laughed. "Hire someone to dig up ground under our own house?"

"You can laugh, but it's not going to be me doing the shoveling." Jonas shrugged. "She didn't bury her cookbooks down here, that's for sure."

Rafe clenched the shovel. "Never let it be said that Rafe Callahan was afraid to spit in the face of the dev—"

"Hello!" someone called down the basement stairs, and they all jumped a foot.

"Holy crap!" Rafe glanced at his brothers. "It's Pete. Do we tell him what we're doing?"

"Anybody down there?" Pete trotted down the stairs, with Creed and Judah close behind. He peered at them in the dim light. "What the hell are you doing? Conducting a séance?"

Rafe sighed. "We're digging up the dead."

"Bad idea," Judah said. "I vote no."

Creed shook his head. "Nothing good can come of this. Fiona told me once that it was just an old sewer pipe that she and Burke had covered over. Trust me, you do not want to hit a sewer pipe."

Rafe blinked. "He has a point."

"Go on, Rafe," Pete said. "You're the thinker in the family. Figure out the best place to start, and go for it. Pick the head or the feet." He grinned at his brother.

"It's not a body." Rafe felt himself breaking a bit of a sweat just thinking about all his brothers' advice, which ranged from "just do it" to "let sleeping dogs lie." "Hell, what have I got to lose?"

"That's right," Sam said. "Keep thinking those snively thoughts, and then just whale away on that dirt."

Rafe took a deep breath. "Stand back," he said, and with a great thrust he tore into the dirt scar, then jumped back.

Chapter Twelve

"Damn," Sam said, "that was anticlimactic. I was half expecting an oil gusher. Weren't you expecting something dramatic like that?" he asked Jonas.

"At least a banshee to come screaming out of the hole," Jonas agreed. "Keep digging, Rafe."

"Why is it always 'keep digging, Rafe'? You guys are capable of a little dirty work, too." Rafe went for another shovelful, feeling more confident now that the ground had been disturbed. Over and over he thrust, building up a nice pile of dirt beside the hole.

"I bet it's nothing," Creed said. "Probably just dirt that wasn't filled in properly when the house was built."

When the shovel made a sudden thud on impact, Rafe froze.

"Uh-oh," Pete said, "that sounded like wood."

"A wood box," Judah said. "That can't be good. Rather coffinlike, wouldn't you say?"

"That's it," Sam said. "Just fill in the hole, put it all back, and let's remember that we love our wily aunt and would never tell anyone that she kept coffins in the basement." He mopped at his brow. "I feel like I'm watching an old movie. Remember that one with the two crazy little aunts who kept bodies in the basement? I always knew Fiona reminded me of someone." He looked around at his brothers. "I need a whiskey something fierce. Anybody care to join me?"

Rafe leaned the shovel against the wall. "This time I agree with Sam. We fill it in and leave it."

"Now?" Jonas demanded. "Right when we're having our finest Indiana Jones moment?" Squatting, Jonas brushed at the dirt with his palm. Plain pine wood appeared under his fingers, and Jonas wiped his hands and stood. "You know, I think I'll throw my vote in with these other two chickens."

"I'm good with that," Pete said. "I'm pretty sure nothing underground needs to come out."

"We'll just ask her," Judah said, pushing some dirt back into the hole with his boot. "Did any of you geniuses ever think of that?"

"I did, but no one ever listens to me." Rafe filled the hole in, then smoothed it over. "Listen, there's only one solution to this tangle. You guys finish up, okay? I've got something to do."

He heard murmurs of protest as he left, but uncovering the wooden footlocker thing had cleared his brain. They'd spent too much time living in the past.

It was time to think only of the future—whether Julie agreed or not.

RAFE BANGED ON HER DOOR twenty minutes later, making enough racket to raise the county. "Julie! We've got to talk!"

The door was opened by a small elderly woman whose blue eyes sparkled behind polka-dotted glasses. "Hello, Rafe."

"Hello, Mrs. Abernathy."

Two more faces appeared behind her. "And Mrs. Waters, Mrs. Night." Rafe took off his hat. "Is there a Books'n'Bingo Society meeting I'm interrupting?"

"Not today." Corinne Abernathy opened the door. "Julie's

asleep. She told us not to let you in. So you'll tell her that the door was open and you thought it was all right to pop in for a quick visit."

"Thanks." Rafe nodded. "What's going on?"

"She's been put on complete bed rest." Nadine Waters smiled at him. "Don't worry. It's pretty normal with triplets."

Rafe gulped, his heart rate jumping. "She was fine when I last saw her."

"Yes," Mavis Night said, "but she started having some cramps. The doctor gave her a shot and told her she's to stay absolutely still for the next three months."

Rafe blinked. "Are the babies all right?"

"They're fine," Corinne said, "as long as she does what she's told."

Rafe looked at Corinne. "I'm surprised Julie would let you in, considering what happened with Sabrina and Seton."

"Don't you worry about my nieces," Corinne said airily. "Julie knows her father can be a pip."

"I don't think she knows that," Rafe said. "We'd been discussing her father, and—"

"I know all about it," Corinne said, brushing his words away. "Fiona had a right to protect her family, and Seton and Sabrina were only doing their jobs. They didn't know Julie then." She smiled at him. "Julie forgives easily."

"She doesn't forgive me," Rafe said, pretty torn up about it.

The ladies all smiled. "Probably not," Corinne said. "Julie's asked us to be her daily help. Not all at once, of course. One of us will be here every day. You'll have plenty of time to consider how you're going to get your family under one roof."

"Any advice?" Rafe was open to suggestions that might help.

"We don't do advice," Mavis said.

Rafe looked at them. "Can I see her?"

"We wouldn't advise it at the moment," Nadine said. "That's the only advice we have."

Rafe shook his head. "If you don't mind, I'm going to go up there and talk to her. I'll say you three were in the garden and had no idea I had come in the door. Deal?"

Corinne nodded. "Five minutes only. This is a serious situation."

"I know. Thanks." He went upstairs to Julie's room, slowly opening the door. "Julie?"

"Go away." She tossed a pillow his direction. "You and your family are bad news."

"Probably." Rafe approached the bed, noting her tired face and pale skin. "How do you feel?"

"Scared."

He pulled a chair up next to the bed so he could sit for a second. "I saw the ladies in the garden, but they—"

"I heard the whole thing. There's no rug on the stairs and sound travels, particularly your deep voice."

"I had to see you." Rafe picked up her hand, which felt cold to him. "Julie, I'm sorry about everything."

"It doesn't matter, does it?" She turned her gaze away.

Rafe took a deep breath. "Julie, marry me."

That got her attention. "Are you crazy?"

"Yes. Julie, listen. It doesn't have to be a forever thing. It doesn't have to be a romantic thing. But let's get married so that the babies will have the best start we can give them."

She raised her brows. "Marrying you is the best start?"

"Yes. I know you don't have a whole lot of reason to trust me right now, but we need to do this for the children."

"Not really. And don't start with the father's-last-name machismo. Jenkins is a fine last name, a better last name in this town than Callahan."

"Julie, think about it." He placed his hand over his heart. "I promise to give you a divorce as soon as you want it."

"I don't want to get married."

"I know. But just consider it. We can have the judge come marry us here."

Julie shook her head slowly. "Even if I wanted to marry you, which I don't, no woman wants to get married in her nightgown, Rafe."

Even if Julie got dressed, she wouldn't want to be married in her bedroom. This was a problem, because there was no way of getting her up and down those steep stairs. "I have to go," he said. "I know this wasn't the most romantic proposal, but it comes from my heart."

"You just want Rancho Diablo. And to stick your finger in my father's eye."

"No," Rafe said, "trust me, I could not care less about any of that. The ranch—heaven only knows what will happen with that. I don't even care anymore. I care about you and these children, and that's my job."

He got up to leave. Julie's eyes followed him as he went to the door. "Julie Jenkins, you're never going to believe this, but I've loved you ever since you drew those fifty red hearts on my face in indelible ink."

A brief smile tried to flit across her face, but she wouldn't let it. "You're right, I don't believe you."

"It's true."

"What's gotten into you?" Julie asked.

Rafe thought about the box he'd unearthed. He thought about his brothers, and their aunt, and realized it was all too complicated to explain right now. "Nothing, except I realized I couldn't live in the past. There's nothing back there that matters. So I'm hanging my hat on the future."

It was true, whether Julie wanted to believe it or not. He put his hat on and departed, leaving his heart in her hands.

JULIE WAS ASTOUNDED BY Rafe's proposal. As she listened to his boots clomping down the steep wooden staircase, she thought about everything he'd said. Did she want to marry him?

"Not exactly," she murmured. "Not just because I'm pregnant."

Her father would be furious. He'd probably have a stroke. But a lot of what Rafe said made sense.

Secretly, Julie knew the truth of what was in her heart, what she wouldn't tell a soul.

She got out of bed and went to the window, pushing it open to look down at Rafe, who was walking to his truck. "Hey!"

He glanced up at the window, did a double take when he saw her standing there. "Get back in bed, damn it!"

He disappeared, and a moment later she heard his boots thundering on the stairs before he burst into her room. She dived into the sheets, covering herself up to her neck.

"Have you ever heard of a cell phone?" he demanded. "I have one in my pocket at all times. Don't get out of this bed again unless it's necessary."

"It was necessary. Don't tell me what to do."

He glared at her, and she glared back.

"Well, I won't say I didn't enjoy the sight of you in your nightie bellowing at me from the window," Rafe said. "I just prefer that the whole neighborhood doesn't enjoy said experience."

"Anyway," Julie said, ignoring him, "I accept your proposal. Not that I forgive you in the least for what you and your family did to mine, but I accept your proposal, considering my children."

"You do?" Rafe sounded shocked, and Julie felt smug that she'd surprised him so much.

"On one condition," she said.

"Anything. Name it."

"Two, actually."

"Whatever. The moon and the stars. Just get on with it."

Julie smiled. "You put the divorce agreement in writing. Have Sam draw up the papers stating that you promise to divorce me without any Callahan shenanigans as soon as I pick a date after the births."

"Why Sam?"

"I'm well aware that Sam is a fine lawyer," Julie said. "I know that if he draws up the papers, they'll be airtight."

"Great," Rafe said. "You trust my brother, but not me."

"Sam's ethical, even if he is a Callahan. I'm hiring him to do this job, and I know he'll do it right. Plus, as your brother, he'll pound you if you try to weasel out of the divorce."

"All right," Rafe said, not sounding happy about it. "What else?"

"I'm not getting married in my bed."

His brows rose. "I can't do much about doctor's orders, Julie."

"You'll figure something out." She smiled. "Aren't you supposed to be the genius in your family?"

"Yeah, but…" He glanced at her stomach, then outside her room. "Why'd you buy a two-story?"

"I wanted this house, Rafe."

He put his hands up at her cool tone. "All right. Let me think for a moment. A small adjustment to your house would have to be made."

"Small? How small?"

"I don't know. I'm going to have to think. You've presented me with a Gordian knot. And yet I've always loved a puzzle, my bountifully plump turtledove." Rafe glanced at her. "I accept all the terms. Do we have a deal?"

After a long moment, Julie nodded.

"Good." Rafe bounded over to the bed and gave her a nice

juicy kiss on the mouth before she could gather her wits to protest. "One week from now, you will be Mrs. Rafe Callahan. Doesn't that have a nice ring to it?"

Julie looked at him. "I'll always be Judge Jenkins, Rafe."

"Sounds good to me."

He strode from the room. Julie watched him go, a little startled that he'd given in so easily. She sank back on her pillows. It was the right thing to do, the practical thing to do. Everyone would be astonished, and happy for her—except her father. She couldn't think about that right now. Rafe had come to her, smelling faintly of earth, and with a dark smear of mud across one cheek, and she'd known that his proposal had been born of the moment. Something had been bothering him.

Both of them knew that the past would always be between them. There was no changing that.

The hardest part of being in love was falling in love with the absolutely most wrong man for her. And yet she'd always had a thing for Rafe Callahan.

She'd have to give him up as soon as the babies were born, though. There was no way to make the past right, because it was too deep, too strong.

May seemed a long way off.

THE NEXT DAY, RAFE CAME into Julie's room looking like a man with a lot of secrets.

"Why are you grinning at me?" Julie asked, her radar already up. "That's how you used to smirk at me in court, and it never failed to annoy me."

"That's okay." Rafe pulled the wooden chair next to her bed and handed her a box. "I can put up with my little woman's moods."

Julie glared at him. "What's this?" she asked, her gaze moving from his handsome face—which she could have looked at for hours, not that she'd ever admit that—to the gold-wrapped box.

"A small token of my affection." Rafe continued smiling at her as if he'd won bingo. "Very small. But expressive."

"I don't want anything from you."

"Not true. You want my name, which I'm giving you gladly."

"No," she said. "Let me remind you I'm keeping my name. Your name is for my children."

"*Our* children. Open."

She was excited to have a gift, though she wouldn't swell his head by telling him. "There's nothing in here."

"There's not?" Rafe peered into the box, pretending to be surprised. "Makes sense, doesn't it?"

"I'm not sure," Julie said, becoming aware that Rafe was having a small laugh at her expense. "Perhaps to you."

He kissed her hand. "I must say I adore you, Julie Jenkins. I love it when you try to act all stiff and schoolteachery, and then go little girl on me."

"You're an ass," Julie said, setting the box on her bedside table.

He handed her another box, this one more delicate than the other. "An even smaller token of my affection."

Julie looked at him. "Why do you go to all this trouble?"

"Because you're so cute when you're annoyed. I always thought that when we were in court. I could sit there for hours watching you purse your lips as you deliberated."

"All right, cowboy, enough with the flattery." She tore into the box, finding a jeweler's box inside. "Now you're just being cruel. This is a Callahan prank, right?"

"You'll have to open it to find out."

He was incorrigible. Still, Julie opened the box. She gasped at the heart-shaped diamond ring nestled in velvet. "Oh, my goodness!"

"Yeah," Rafe said, "that's what I said when I saw the price tag."

She stared at the ring, practically afraid to touch it. "It's… ostentatious, don't you think?"

Rafe grinned. "Yep. Just like my lady."

Julie raised a brow. "How do you figure?"

He leaned back in the wooden chair, pleased with himself. "Well, three babies right off the bat impressed me. So I told the jeweler to make it three carats, one for each baby. If you can't find a stone that size in that shape, then make a diamond band for it."

Julie shook her head. "This is too much."

"Don't you like the ring?" Rafe looked worried.

"I do. What woman wouldn't?" She closed the lid, fighting temptation. "But we're not really going to be married, except on paper. And we're getting divorced. I don't need a ring like this, Rafe."

He patted her hand. "I never realized you're a thinker, too." He smiled at her, his eyes kind. "This will be good for our children."

Julie was dying to try on the ring. "It's a lot of money to spend—"

He pulled the ring from the box and slid it on her finger. Checking it from every angle, he seemed to decide it suited him. Then he pressed her hand to his lips, making her heart jump like crazy. "Don't worry, angel cake. It's not real. A pretend ring for a fake marriage. Pretty smart, huh?"

"Oh," Julie said. "I see." Her heart sank to her stomach. "Yes. It is smart."

"Now." Rafe got to his feet and pulled out a tape measure. "I've been working on the problem of getting you downstairs to your living room for our wedding. That's where you want to be married, isn't it?"

"If it could be managed," Julie said.

"I can do anything," Rafe boasted, and she sat back to admire her pretend ring.

"Thank you, Rafe." Trust him to think of a pretend symbol for their temporary marriage. She wished she felt relieved when she thought of being a temporary wife to him, but somehow she didn't. "I do like the ring."

He smiled. "Enough to let me sleep in that bed with you?"

"No," Julie said. "Nice try, though."

He went off whistling, and closed her door. She heard him moving around on the landing, muttering to himself. It sounded as if he was measuring something, because she heard a metal tape extend, then snap shut. Occasionally, she thought she heard a disgruntled curse or two. Then the tape measure snapped shut a final time. "I'll be going now, beautiful!" Rafe called. "Try not to miss me too much!"

"I won't!"

The front door slammed, and Julie took off the ring, inspecting it from every angle. It was the most stunning thing she'd ever seen. The diamond was so big she'd feel flashy wearing it—and yet it was so pretty, with the heart shape, that she couldn't help admiring it.

It was fake. "Fine with me," she said. "I wouldn't have expected anything else from a Callahan."

She looked in the band, found "950 plat" inscribed there, and gasped. The ring was in no way fake—it was platinum, which meant the diamond was real, too. And expensive.

That was the problem with Rafe. She never knew when he was serious, or when he was just being a Callahan.

He didn't want her to feel forced or rushed into something she didn't want, obviously, given the elaborate presentation he'd gone through, first with the empty "joke" box and then the "fake" ring.

Yet Julie knew one serious thing about Rafe now: he was very intent on marrying her.

It was the children he wanted.

She slipped the ring back on, wondering if it was all right to be falling just a little bit in love with a Callahan, in spite of knowing how much it would hurt later on when it all ended.

It was too late now to wonder about that. She'd just have to keep pretending.

Chapter Thirteen

When Rafe arrived the next day, he brought backup. The only way to keep his easily alarmed fiancée from figuring out what he was up to was to keep her mind on other things.

Therefore, he pressed his five brothers into service. Sam and Jonas would help him with the installation. Pete, Judah and Creed would entertain Julie with tales of his heroic exploits.

It would take some finesse, but finesse he and his brothers had in spades.

"What's he doing out there?" Rafe heard Julie ask.

He looked at his brothers. "You see what I'm up against. She's such a distrustful lady. We'll have to make quick work of this if I'm going to marry her in five days."

"No pressure or anything," Sam said.

Rafe handed Jonas a piece of mahogany. "I figure this has got to be strong enough to hold a man who weighs two hundred pounds, just for safety's sake."

Julie's squeal of protest could be heard in the next state. "Creed, shut that door!" Rafe yelled.

"Whew," he muttered when the door was closed. "Remind me not to mention weight around the judge again."

Sam laughed. "Never mention it around any woman you're trying to sleep with."

"Yeah, well." Rafe let that go. Julie didn't seem in any

mood to let him into her bed. He really couldn't blame her. Unless he played his cards very well, the doghouse was going to be his abode for the duration of their short marriage. "Now, for the motor."

Judah poked his head into the hall. "She's trying to come out."

"She has to stay in bed. Doc's orders."

Sam and Jonas looked worried. Judah's expression was one of panic.

"The judge says you better not be messing up her beautiful house," Judah told him.

Rafe sighed. "How does she expect me to get her downstairs? Shove her out the window onto a trampoline?"

Another shriek pierced the air.

"Damn," Jonas said, "didn't you tell her what you were installing?"

"No," Rafe said. "The chariot is none of her business."

"You're a thickheaded prince." Sam grinned. "I'll never follow your example."

"Good idea." To Judah, Rafe said, "Did you give her the chocolates?"

"Forgot about that!" Judah slammed the door.

"If everyone would just follow orders, this would be a piece of cake." Rafe eyed the pine banister, satisfied that in about ten minutes the hideous old pine would be replaced by the purposeful and stronger new mahogany.

"So when are you going to tell her about the chief and the mineral rights?" Sam asked.

"I'm not. That's your job. File it." Rafe measured carefully. He was pretty proud of thinking how to best get his angel down these hideous stairs, and at the moment that was all he intended to worry about. "Now, roll that Oriental rug down the stairs, Jonas. Let's see if it's long enough to cover this ugly staircase."

The rug fit the wooden stairs like a dream. "Like *Architectural Digest*," Rafe said, proud of himself. "Let's fasten the brass attachments, and that's stage one complete."

"There's not a woman on the planet who likes it when a man butts his nose into her decorating," Jonas said.

"She assigned me the job of getting her downstairs safely, and that's what I'm going to do." He looked at the wall, measuring the handrail again for the hundredth time. "All right, Sam, let's unscrew this ugly thing and put this beauty on."

Pete poked his head out. "Julie says you'd better not make so much as a mark on her *beautiful* house."

"I'm not." Rafe didn't even look up from his measuring. "Tell Rapunzel she either goes down the stairs my way or marries me in her bed. Her choice."

Judah stuck his head out. "Julie says she's changed her mind about marrying you, if you're doing something to her staircase. She says it's the reason she bought this house."

"Lovely," Rafe muttered. "Shut the door."

They did, and he pulled the handrail off the wall. "Like a dream," he said, "which is what proper measuring does for a project. Now, the new one."

"It's a vast improvement," Jonas said, holding the long piece of rounded mahogany, while Sam and Rafe each fitted an end. With the first *zzz!* of the electric screwdriver, a shriek curdled Rafe's bravado.

"Damn, she sounds bloodthirsty, bro," Jonas said. "The judge is going to have your head."

"It's all right. I've had nightmares about my munchkins falling down this staircase. Everybody knows stairs and kids go together. This one's going to be as safe as I can make it, regardless of little mama in there."

Jonas and Sam looked at him.

"You may not stay married long with that attitude," Sam said.

"I probably won't stay married long, anyway, but that's a problem for another day. This is rock solid." He looked with satisfaction at the beautiful rug on the stairs and the wonderful hand-carved handrail he'd bought from an artisan. "Now, let's get to the fancy part. We don't have much longer before she tears down that door."

Jonas and Sam sprang into action faster than he'd ever seen them move. It was now or never for his grand plan.

This was the only way to get his bride to the altar to say I do.

He pulled out the pieces of the magic chariot and began.

"IF WE WERE IN COURT," Julie said, "I'd hold all three of you in contempt."

"We know," Judah said. "Trust me, we're nervous as hell, Your Honor."

"I'm going to that door." Julie glared at Creed and Pete. "I'm going *out* that door. You will not stop me."

"It's not a good idea, Judge," Pete said, looking rather sickly for a man who was once considered one of the hottest bachelors in town.

"It's like Christmas. No peeking," Creed said, sounding worried. "Let's look at that fake ring our brother bought you. Does it fit? Can he get anything right?"

"Don't worry about my ring. Out of my way." Julie rose from the bed, glad she'd put on a pretty dress before Rafe had shown up with his crew.

They parted before her like a little boy's wet hair under a wide-toothed comb. She flung open the door.

Her jaw dropped.

Rafe looked up at her, his expression proud.

She stared at the chair attached to the wall. "What is *that?*"

"This," Rafe said, "is the first automated chair genie in

Diablo. I promised I'd get you downstairs for our wedding. And I always keep my promises."

Julie blinked. Looked back at the new rug, which she had to admit was lovely, and the new rail, a thing of beauty—and the awful chair thing. "When I said I wanted you to get me downstairs for the wedding, Rafe," she said, "I was sort of hoping you'd carry me."

His eyes went wide. His gaze bounced to her stomach and back to her face. "Carry you?"

"Down the stairs and back up." Julie looked at the motorized chair lift and wanted to cry. It was practical. She knew it made sense. In fact, it was a great idea. Rafe couldn't carry her down the stairs. Especially not these stairs, which were pretty steep.

It was so practical it made her mad.

She burst into tears, and the brothers scattered. She'd never seen five men run down a flight of stairs so fast; it sounded like thunder on the rug-covered steps. They hit the front door without looking back.

"Everything all right up there?" Corinne Abernathy asked. Her doughy face and polka-dotted glasses appeared at the bottom of the stairwell. "I almost have your dinner ready, Julie. Oh, look. Isn't that lovely? Now I have a way to get up the stairs without worrying about falling. You'll have to show me how to work that contraption, Rafe."

Corinne went back into the kitchen, and Julie went to bed.

"Julie," Rafe said, going to her bedside, and she waved a tissue at him.

"You always go overboard," she told him. "That's the problem. It can't ever be a small ring, or that you simply carry me. You have to do everything huge."

"Well, yeah. And may I remind you that you're the one who's having triplets. That's not exactly small, you know." He got into bed beside her, pulling off his boots and letting them fall to the floor before he collapsed on her white comforter. "Did I ever tell you that this is the softest bed in the world?"

"How would you know?" Julie blew her nose ungracefully.

"Just a hunch." He turned his head and smiled at her. "Tell the truth. You love the chariot. See, it's a *chair*-iot so you'll know it's romantic. I don't want you to feel like it didn't come straight from my heart."

"You're an idiot," Julie said, blowing her nose again, "and I don't love it. But it is a good idea. Let the record reflect I admit that with prejudice. I do not want that thing in my darling little house."

"Duly noted."

"Still," Julie said, "I see the practicality of it."

"That's my girl." He sounded distinctly sleepy. Julie realized he'd worn himself out putting the "chair-iot" in. She scooched down on her pillow and closed her eyes, wondering how many men would think of such a gadget for their pregnant fiancée.

Probably not many.

Rafe was smart, and she admired that about him.

He was a rascal, and in spite of herself, she admired that, too.

"Thank you, Rafe," she said, but he was already sound asleep.

Julie smiled, and snuggled up to her cowboy while he was too unconscious to know that she was giving in—just a little.

RAFE GOT UP CAREFULLY so he wouldn't wake Julie. She slept like a woman expecting triplets should—hard. And she was a bed hog. Another thing he'd learned about his quickly growing lady.

He went out to the hallway, examined his handiwork and decided to take it for a spin to the bottom of the staircase. Then he rode it back up, listening for any squeak or sound that might indicate it needed an adjustment.

"Perfect," he murmured. "If only women were as easy as gadgets."

"I heard that!"

Rafe grinned at Julie's voice and went down to find Corinne in the kitchen. "When you're ready, I'll show you how to use the chariot, Corinne."

She waved a potholder at him and handed him a sack. "There's your dinner. Your brothers said you do all the cooking now."

"It's true. Mostly chops and stuff. They don't complain." They didn't dare.

"How are you doing now that your aunt is gone? We miss Fiona so much."

Rafe shrugged. "It's not easy. We miss her and Burke, too."

"We need a new president of the Books'n'Bingo Society. But we don't want to elect just anyone. Fiona was always so full of energy."

Rafe nodded. "I know. Maybe we'll hear from her soon."

"In the meantime, what are you going to do about Julie's father?"

Rafe frowned. "Do about him?"

Corinne gazed at him, her blue eyes huge. "Every girl wants her father to walk her down the aisle."

"Oh." Rafe stared at Corinne. "Ah, that would be Julie's department, wouldn't it? I don't dare interfere with whatever those two have decided."

"He's difficult. Horrible, even. But he is her father. He'll be your father-in-law, and grandfather to your children." Corinne smiled gently at him. "You're such a clever young man, Rafe. Your mother was always so proud of you. I'm sure you'll think of something."

"My mother?" Rafe was startled.

"Well, yes." Corinne looked surprised. "She did live here, you know. She used to bring you boys into town."

This was the first time he could recall anyone talking about his parents. They'd been gone before he'd been old enough to realize that his was not a normal family. When he'd asked about a mother and father, first the brothers had been told they'd gone away. Later, that they'd gone to heaven.

"Well," Corinne said, patting him on the arm, "you think about it. Families come in all shapes and sizes, you know. And life is shorter than we think it is. It's best to start a marriage off on the best foot possible."

Rafe nodded. Then he left, not wanting to think anymore about Bode. The man was a troublemaker. Even Julie couldn't manage him.

Inviting him to the wedding would be inviting disaster.

Nothing was getting in the way of Rafe getting Julie to say I do. There was too much at stake.

It was a miracle she'd agreed to marry him, even for a short while.

No one could blame Rafe if he didn't ask Bode for his daughter's hand in marriage. The man was evil, he'd made Fiona's life a nightmare and nearly got their ranch.

Not a chance in hell will I invite him—not even for Julie.

Chapter Fourteen

Rafe was taking over her life.

He had to, because, he said, she needed to focus on her pregnancy and nothing else. She'd endured him sending someone to the house to take her blood, draw up the license—all doable, Rafe said, because of her position as a well-respected judge—and she was pretty certain he'd redecorated her entire downstairs. Every day for the past week, Julie had heard all types of noises coming from the living room, no matter how quiet everyone tried to be.

Now it was the big day.

He'd had his sisters-in-law Jackie and Darla come fit her in a gown they'd brought from their wedding shop.

"It's a caftan," Julie said, and Darla laughed.

"But a lovely caftan." Jackie smiled at Julie. "You're lucky the doctor says you can stand for the five minutes it takes to say I do. Otherwise, Rafe would haul Judge Pearson upstairs to get you married."

"I know." Julie didn't exactly appreciate the knowledge that, where once she'd had a lot of power—even over the Callahans—now she was helpless as a baby. "He's annoying."

"He's amazing." Jackie checked the dress for fit one last time. "You're going to be a beautiful bride. Welcome to the family."

Jackie and Darla hugged her, and Julie felt that she had new sisters who understood her predicament. "Whoever heard of a Thanksgiving wedding?" she muttered.

"That's the wedding march," Jackie said. "Let's get you seated on this chariot thing. My daughters are going to scatter rose petals as you come down the, ah, wall. I hope you don't mind."

Julie felt tears prickle her eyes. "What a darling idea. Thank you."

"Thank Rafe. He thinks of everything. He drove us nuts trying to make everything perfect," Jackie said.

Darla nodded. "He's crazy about you, Julie." She placed a bouquet of white roses and pink ribbons in Julie's hand. "You're marrying a great guy."

Julie blinked, about to say *Rafe's not crazy about me,* but they were hustling her into the chair, and Julie was trying to look beautiful and not huge and stressed, so she forgot to argue. The little girls began tossing petals when Jackie told them to, and then, like magic, Julie began to move down the wall. Guests snapped pictures, and tears jumped into Julie's eyes, and when she saw Rafe standing at the bottom of the stairs, so handsome and tall in his tux, she nearly began weeping in earnest.

But then she saw her living room and gasped. It had been transformed into a fairyland of wedding magic. Julie could hardly believe all the flowers and ribbons that had been artfully placed around the fireplace. "It's so beautiful," she said, and Rafe squeezed her hand.

"The Books'n'Bingo Society has been hard at work. I'm no good with flowers." He smiled down at her. "You're gorgeous."

"I'm not," she said, thinking *but* you *are.*

Then she saw her father standing next to the judge. Another gasp escaped her. "How did you get my dad to come?" she asked softly.

Rafe took her hand, helping her to stand up. "I told him I'd beat him to a pulp if he let you down."

Julie looked up at Rafe, not certain if he was serious this time or not. "Did you really?"

"He's here, isn't he?"

Rafe wasn't smiling. Julie had a funny feeling he might be telling the truth. "Thank you, Rafe."

He shrugged. "Don't thank me. I didn't do that out of the kindness of my heart, trust me. I did it for you."

She felt a little forgiveness slide into her soul. Even if his family had planted spies at her house, it seemed as if Rafe was trying to go forward with a clean slate. She wanted so badly to trust him, to put the past behind them.

But then she looked at her father's face—not happy, and certainly resentful—and Julie knew Rafe probably *had* threatened her father if he didn't show up today.

Bode would say that Rafe made him come, not from sentimental reasons, but to lord over him that he was stealing his daughter from him, in front of the fifty guests packed into her living room.

Julie held in a sigh, and let Rafe walk her to the altar.

The I do's were said within five minutes, Julie was allowed to see the lovely table the Books'n'Bingo Society ladies had set up with a wedding cake and cookies for the guests, and she cut the cake with Rafe.

Then she was hustled back up the stairs on her chair. Rafe walked beside her, and the guests threw paper hearts as they went.

"All right, Mrs. Callahan, back in bed you go. Can I help you out of that dress?"

Julie grimaced. "I think I can manage. And please don't call me that."

Rafe kissed her on the nose and unzipped her dress before she realized his hand had searched out her zipper. "I deserve to get as much mileage out of your new name as possible, since I had to call you Judge Jenkins for so long."

"I don't feel like being teased about it, Rafe." She didn't feel married. The babies were moving around like mad inside her—so active it felt as if her stomach were a jungle gym. "Arghh, I think my children know they didn't get a piece of wedding cake." She got into bed, moving slowly.

"Do you want some cake?" Rafe asked.

"No, thank you. They don't need sugar. Until you've had some of Corinne's cake, you don't know what high octane is. Her cake is the stuff of sugar heaven, and my babies would be bouncing around all day."

He looked at her as she pulled the pins out of her hair. "You're the most beautiful bride I've ever seen. And I've seen a lot lately."

An unwilling smile crossed Julie's face. "Go enjoy the guests. I'm going to nap."

"I'd rather enjoy you."

"Well, I don't see that happening in your near future." The words came out more snarky than she intended, and Julie instantly looked at Rafe. "I didn't mean that quite the way it sounded."

"Talk about dashing a guy's hopes." He kissed her and went down the stairs whistling the wedding march. Julie sighed, slightly resentful that her party was downstairs and she was up here. Still, it had been a lovely wedding—except for her father.

He was never going to understand. But she was doing what she had to do.

"THE LAST GUEST IS GONE." Rafe fell into bed next to Julie, still wearing his tux. "There's a boatload of gifts stacked in one of the bedrooms. My brothers said they were developing great glutes from going up and down the stairs storing your gifts."

"Our gifts," Julie said sleepily, glad Rafe was in bed with her. "No one should have given us anything, considering that was a faux wedding."

"All right, faux bride. I worked my tail off on our wedding. I don't want to hear anything about fakery." Rafe patted her hand, and then his palm stole over to her abdomen. "You'll probably want to keep me before this is all over."

"Whoever heard of a Thanksgiving wedding?" Julie murmured yet again. "It can't be lucky."

"That reminds me. The ladies left a turkey and a potato casserole in the fridge for you." He opened his eyes and looked at her. "Hungry?"

Julie shook her head. "Tell me how you got my father here, Rafe. I want to know the story."

Rafe sighed. "Must we talk about warlocks when we could be discussing your handsome prince?"

"Yes."

"All right." He shrugged. "My brothers and I rounded him up. Just like you would a bull. We penned him in his house, gave him his options, and then I assured him that if he so much as made you cry at your wedding, I'd give him a thrashing he'd never forget."

Julie couldn't help feeling sorry for her elderly father. "Rafe, he's old and not in good health."

Rafe waved a hand. "Julie, I promise you, he's mean as a snake and going to live forever drinking the nectar of bitterness. He's fine."

She pursed her lips, imagining her small, wiry father

being set on by six beefy Callahans. "Do you always have to get your way?"

"Yeah." Rafe picked up her hand, kissing her fingertips one by one without opening his eyes. "Remember that."

She pulled her hand away. "Not a day goes by that I don't."

"Good. Now go to sleep. Tell my children to sleep. Let's all wake up tomorrow and eat turkey and stuffing."

He was snoring a moment later. Julie glanced over at her new husband. He hadn't kissed her like a real bride usually was kissed, nor told her he loved her.

"I've got myself in a real pickle," Julie muttered.

"Did you say pickle?" Rafe demanded groggily. "You want pickles and ice cream?"

Julie flopped a pillow over Rafe's handsome face. Snores burst from underneath, and she shook her head.

I'm married.

What am I going to do with him?

FROM THE DAY SHE GOT married, Julie's life changed. When she said she felt awkward about Corinne helping in the house so much because her nieces had been spying on her, Rafe said spying was an art form, and wondered if Corinne could teach him the skill.

Julie had thrown her knitting at him. Mavis had been teaching her to knit. Knitting was not meant for impatient judges, but Rafe said she should probably make him a pair of socks as a wedding gift. He'd said it in a smug tone, as if he didn't think she could do it, so Julie set her mind to learning to knit—though she assured him she'd rather stab him with her shiny new knitting needles.

He didn't spend much time with her during the day, but every night, he rubbed her stomach before falling asleep. Julie told him her stomach was not a pumpkin to be manhandled, and Rafe said that anything that large ought to be given a blue ribbon at the state fair.

She'd seriously thought about using her knitting needles as weapons then, eyeing them on her bedside table with relish.

On Christmas Eve, Rafe brought her a plate of turkey and a present.

She looked at him, already leery of the grin he wore.

"It's a book," she guessed.

"But what kind?" he asked. "Open it."

She did, not impressed with the baby name book. "I don't want to think about names."

"That's fine," Rafe said. "We can just use family names for my sons. Like Rafael Peter, or Jonas Creed—"

"Did I not tell you?" Julie asked, keeping her tone light.

"Tell me what?" Rafe looked at her, his handsome face wreathed with concern.

"You're having daughters, cowboy. Three of them."

Rafe's expression was comical. He sank onto the bed, staring at her. "Girls?"

Julie nodded. "Mmm."

"All of them?"

"Every one." She patted his hand. "Just for you."

Rafe laughed out loud. "That's awesome."

She looked at him, fully expecting a completely different reaction. "It is?"

He hopped over the bed and took her face in his hands, giving her the kind of kiss she'd hoped he'd give her when they got married. "Julie Jenkins, that's a jackpot. Three stars, all the way across. Triple judges."

"You're weird," Julie said, pulling back from him. "I thought you'd be disappointed."

"My sweet lamb chop. Nothing about you disappoints me." He kissed her hand, then her stomach, then kissed her lips, so deeply her ears rang. "Julie, you were keeping that a secret, weren't you?"

She sniffed. "Just hoping to take you down a peg or two."

He rubbed his palms together. "This is going to be great. You realize what this means, don't you?"

He was just too happy for his own good. "What does it mean?"

"It means," Rafe said, "we'll have three candidates for FFA Sweetheart."

She blinked. "They might be tomboys. They might be cheerleaders."

"I get three little Julies," Rafe said, ignoring her trying to burst his bubble, as he usually did. "Jackpot!"

He went off whistling again, and Julie flounced against the pillows. It was just too easy to fall in love with him. She was falling hard, too hard.

And it was much too late to stop now.

May births meant a May divorce.

Julie picked up her knitting—the sock had become a sleeve—and ignored the baby name book.

It would serve him right to have to pick out the girl names. Maybe he'd realize that life with four women wasn't going to be a matter to whistle about all the time.

"I feel like an incubator," she groused, "thanks to that Christmas turkey!"

ON CHRISTMAS DAY, RAFE brought her a giant slice of tenderloin, brown rice, sweet potato pie and no fudge, which she knew very well had been made by Nadine Waters and passed out to all her friends. The Callahans would have received a pound of the luscious dark fudge sprinkled with pecans.

Rafe fell into the wooden chair across from her bed after delivering the Christmas tray. "You said the babies couldn't have sugar. Nadine's fudge is all sugar."

"True." Julie was big as a house now, and a piece of fudge was uppermost in her mind. Could it hurt to add to the weight at this point? "But I know how good it is, so if you don't bring me a piece, I'll probably make you wear your Christmas present."

He raised a brow. "The sweater?"

"Don't sound so snide." She pointed to the knitted pile, which was a horrible, misshapen beginner's attempt. "Once you put it on, you'll love it."

"I absolutely will." A shadow crossed his face from out of nowhere. "This is such a strange Christmas without Fiona."

Julie put her fork down, surprised. Rafe never had down moments. "I'm so sorry," she said, before she realized she probably shouldn't be sorry at all. Since Fiona had left, her father had calmed down quite a bit. He was still ornery—especially since the marriage—but he wasn't running around all the time mad as a hornet.

Rafe shrugged. "We didn't have a Christmas party this year. We've had those since before we could remember. It's part of the Callahan tradition. My brothers and I had to put up the Christmas lights this year, and I can't tell you what a chore that is. I always knew Fiona did the work of ten people, but I don't think I realized I couldn't keep up with her."

"It's because you're running two households." Julie felt guilty about that.

He'd fallen asleep, his head rolled back against the wall. Here he was, day after day, taking care of her, feeding her, amusing her.

All because she'd secretly always had a thing for Rafe Callahan, and couldn't keep her dress down around him.

It felt vaguely dishonest. And when he'd talked about how much he missed Fiona, and how different their Christmas was with her gone, pain flashed through Julie. Fiona had left because of Bode.

Bode wasn't even speaking to Julie.

Something had to give.

There was no way a real marriage could be built on such a shaky foundation.

Chapter Fifteen

Rafe woke up, his neck seriously crinked from falling asleep in the wooden chair in Julie's room. "I'm replacing this damn chair, Julie. It's killing me."

And something came over his turtledove. It was as if fire shot from her pretty brunette head. "You're not changing another thing in my house," she snapped. "In fact, I don't want you staying here anymore, Rafe."

He looked at her. "Of course I'm staying with you. You're my wife. Why wouldn't I stay with my family?"

Julie glared at him like an avenging princess. "Your family is at Rancho Diablo."

"It's Christmas, Julie. You don't want to kick Santa Claus out." He was dying to show her what he'd done downstairs. And what he'd done to the girls' nursery.

He was pretty certain he'd mastered the art of pleasing a woman by decorating. "Besides, I want my Christmas sweater."

"I haven't finished it. And I'm not going to."

Julie sounded mad about something, real mad. Rafe went through the files in his brain quickly. He'd come in, they'd made small talk, he'd fallen asleep... "Oh," he said, grinning, "you think I forgot your Christmas present. You greedy little girl."

Fire did spark from her eyes. "I don't want a present, I want you to go back where you belong."

Now Rafe was really confused. His lady never turned down a present. "Chocolates?"

"No."

Well, hell, if chocolate candy wasn't going to soothe her, he really was in the soup. "You know, this wooden chair isn't so bad—"

"Go."

Maybe it was a hormone thing. Could be a holiday thing, Rafe mused. Some folks got moody around this time of year. And it couldn't be easy being cooped up in here when she'd probably rather be running around town doing her judge thing and spreading holiday cheer. He scratched at his head. "Will you call me if you need something?"

"I'll call my father."

"Oh." Rafe stepped back. "Uh, did he come by?"

"No," Julie said, and Rafe said, "Oh."

So she was having misgivings because of the holidays. He understood. Julie had been through a lot in a short amount of time. "All right. I'm going. But just remember, it's Christmas, and you could have had Santa."

She waved at him, not falling for it.

So he left, pretty certain everybody loved Santa—except his wife.

"AND THEN I WAS OUT, just like that." Rafe flung himself on the sofa in the library, feeling depressed. Sam and Jonas sat commiserating with him, even though he refused the brandy they offered him.

"Well, you got a lot done in a short amount of time. Think of it that way," Sam said.

"Why?" Rafe felt as if his relationship with Julie was moving at turtle speed.

"One day we were digging up the basement, and suddenly you ran out to shanghai Julie. I mean, think about it." Sam shrugged. "Whatever ghost you stirred up, at least you got yourself a bride."

"Yeah." Rafe was puzzled by Julie's about-face. "I think Bode's at the bottom of this."

"Bode's at the bottom of everything," Jonas said, tranquil for the moment as he sipped his brandy. "Did you ever tell her about the mineral rights? The tribe? She's not going to like you too much when she finds out you weren't honest with her."

Rafe winced. "I've made it a policy not to discuss Rancho Diablo with Julie. Why should I? We're still being sued by her father."

"I was wondering how that was working." Sam shook his head. "I foresee troubled waters ahead for you, bro. I do see your side, in fact I'm impressed by your ability to compartmentalize." He poured himself more brandy, and then a snifter for Rafe. "I just don't think your wife's going to be all that impressed."

"Yeah, well." Rafe took the snifter, sipped, then sighed. "She claims she's not really my wife."

Jonas and Sam stared at him.

"I think that's a first in our family," Sam said.

"You're telling me." Rafe was pretty hurt by that. All the Callahan brides had seemed happy to be at the altar with his brothers.

"You and Julie did start from a different place." Jonas nodded at him. "It'll probably all work out eventually. Right now, Julie's got all kinds of things happening to her."

"Yeah." Rafe knew that. It didn't make it easier.

"And while we're on this subject," Sam said, "there's something I've been meaning to mention."

Jonas and Rafe looked at him. Sam cleared his throat.

"My suggestion, acting as legal counsel for Rancho Diablo, is that we countersue Bode."

"Nuts," Rafe said. "That won't go over well with my wife." He could think of nothing worse.

"What are you thinking, Sam?" Jonas asked.

"Bode's got a team of lawyers who spend their lives drawing this thing out. It's motion after motion. The problem is that, even with me heading up our legal team, it's running into some stiff money. As you know, Bode will never be convinced that he didn't best Fiona financially. He thinks he caught her square in his net."

"Are we planning to reveal that the mineral rights are not part of our ranch?" Jonas asked.

"If Rafe hasn't told Julie—"

"I haven't," Rafe snapped at Sam. "The last thing I want to do is remind my wife why she hates me so much."

"Then I suggest at the first of the year we drop the bomb on Bode," Sam said. "To try to convince him that we're tired of monkeying around with him, and hopefully, to get this suit wound up."

Rafe blinked. "On what grounds?"

"Harassment, for starters. Think of how many times he's come over here threatening us," Sam stated. "We should file that his claims are unsubstantiated, and that the State can't take property that is a family dwelling. Many dwellings now, in fact. The State never wanted this ranch until Bode egged his buddies on to take it." Sam drew a deep breath. "Contrary to his lawsuit trying to take our ranch, I suggest we sue for his. I discovered, for one thing, that his fence line is ten feet over on our side."

"Crap," Rafe said. Sam was really sharpening the ax.

"Aerial snapshots also reveal that his livestock regularly encroach on our land. They're clearly marked, and we don't have the type of steers he has, anyway." Sam held up some photographs. "We'll also claim that since he hasn't paid his taxes for the past five years, his property should go into default."

Rafe sat up. "Sam, you have to be wrong about that."

"Nope." His brother shook his head. "Discovered it when I was looking through some tax liens."

"I wouldn't think anyone could file a lawsuit against someone's property if they're in arrears on their own taxes. He can't have a lawsuit pending if he's currently in debt to Uncle Sam, can he?" Jonas asked.

"He can if his lawyers don't know, and if his daughter's a well-respected judge," Sam said.

"Oh, no," Rafe moaned. "You're sticking pins in my marriage."

"We have to do whatever it takes to save Rancho Diablo," Jonas said. "We fight fire with fire."

"I just don't believe Julie would be that unethical," Rafe argued, "even for her father's sake."

"I didn't say she knew he was behind in his taxes." Sam held up some papers. "I didn't get these from Seton, by the way."

"You did!" Jonas said. "What the hell?"

"I didn't," Sam insisted. "I don't know where she is right now. Which is your fault," he told Rafe.

"Not really," Rafe said. "Continue."

"These are his tax bills, and what he's behind on." Sam shrugged. "According to tax lawyers I consulted, anyone who's that far behind on taxes and hasn't lost their property has friends in high places. I say we force the issue."

"This is bad." Rafe took a giant swig of his brandy and coughed when it went down the wrong way. "I think I'm going to have to recuse myself from this conversation."

"You can't," Jonas said. "You're one-sixth of the ranch. You're married now, and have three kids on the way. That means your part of the ranch will come out of trust and be fully yours."

"She's never going to forgive me." Rafe looked from Sam to Jonas. "Do we have to do this? Can we wait until after the babies are born? I mean, you don't know the little judge. She's going to throw me out for good."

"When's the due date?" Sam demanded.

"I think May. I don't know. By the size of her, I'd say tomorrow." He groaned. "My angel is going to roast me alive."

"I heard she got rid of Corinne and Nadine and Mavis," Sam said.

"What?" Rafe shot straight up. "How do you know this?"

"I have my sources," Sam said, his face serious.

Rafe was astounded. "She didn't say a word to me. Did they tell you why she did that?"

Sam nodded. "Corinne said that Julie was uncomfortable having them around because Seton and Sabrina are Corinne's nieces. And they were all Fiona's best friends."

"I don't know how she thinks she's going to take care of herself," Rafe said, not liking that decisions were being made without him concerning the welfare of his children.

"She hired a girl from the county to help her." Sam shook his head. "Only at night, though."

Rafe's blood pressure felt as if it might shoot through his head. "I'll be glad when the babies are born."

Jonas frowned. "What does the doc say?"

"That if she doesn't stay still, he's going to give her some kind of IV to keep the babies in." Rafe gulped. "I don't want to talk about this anymore. I'm caught square in the middle."

"Yeah," Sam said, "you'd best figure out a way to get your wife on your side."

"Right," Rafe said, "and chickens are going to fly out of my butt." He took his snifter and went to the kitchen to dig around for some of Nadine's fudge.

Julie was sitting at home by herself, wanting fudge.

He wanted his family.

She'd thrown him out.

He had three daughters on the way who deserved their rightful heritage.

"Crap." Rafe put the fudge down and stared out the window. "It's going to get ugly around here fast."

ON VALENTINE'S DAY, Bode handed his daughter three pink teddy bears. "You look well, daughter."

Julie took the bears. "Nice of you to finally visit, Dad."

"Well, a father worries about his girl, you know." Bode looked at her. "I miss you being in my house, Julie, but I shouldn't have thrown such a tantrum about it. I hope you can forgive me."

She was glad he was here to put the angry words behind them. "There was really nothing to forgive. So much happened so fast that everyone was a little unsettled."

"Yes." Bode nodded. "I'm afraid I didn't act my best when I found out Seton was a plant. I'd grown very fond of her. No one likes to find out that someone they care about doesn't care about them in return."

"No, they don't," Julie murmured.

"Of course, I was also upset that you'd decided to move out. I knew that as soon as you did, Callahan would start hanging around, twisting your mind with lies about me."

"He didn't, Dad." Julie could say that with complete honesty. "We rarely talked about you."

"Well, the Callahans are more subtle than that," Bode said. "He got you pregnant, and that was how he beat me."

Julie looked at her father. "That thought never crossed Rafe's mind."

He laughed. "Trust me, it would cross any man's mind.

You're a rare jewel, Julie, a prize. Any man who got you away from me was going to feel like he'd won the jackpot."

Rafe had called their daughters a jackpot. Julie's skin chilled. "I haven't seen Rafe in a month and a half."

Bode looked at her, not registering surprise. "Is that so?"

She sighed. "Who have you had watching my house?" Just from his tone, and his sudden visit, she knew someone had reported to her father that Rafe hadn't been around. What he didn't know was that she'd kicked Rafe out. Rafe called every day, and every day she told him she didn't want to see him.

She'd been shocked that he'd stayed away. It would be different after his daughters were born. He probably had an army of lawyers teed up, waiting to help him claim custodial rights.

The thought made her mad. "Dad, you need to stay out of my business. Rafe needs to stay out of my business. I love you both, but my life is my life."

"You don't love him," Bode said. "Honey, you don't know what love is. Love is what your mother and I had."

Julie nodded. "I know you loved Mom, Dad."

"I still love her. And I'd have her today if the Callahans—"

"Dad!" Julie couldn't go on hearing another poisonous word. She felt as if she were caught in a tunnel that never seemed to end. "Listen, Dad, I really need to rest. Do you mind going now? It's been great seeing you, but I'm not supposed to have visitors."

Bode jumped to his feet. "Do you need anything?"

Rafe, Julie wanted to say. "No, thanks."

"I'll let myself out."

"Thank you. And take the spy off my house. Rafe's a part of my life you'll have to accept."

Her father gave her a long look.

"If I find out that you don't remove them, you won't see your granddaughters," Julie told him.

She shut her eyes, relieved when she heard the front door close. It was never going to end. Her father's suffering was a terminal thing, something he'd had for so long he couldn't let it go.

Pain sliced across Julie's abdomen, making her gasp.

She waited for the cramping to go away, closing her eyes and willing herself to relax.

The pangs got worse.

An hour later, realizing the pain was becoming more intense, Julie picked up the phone.

Chapter Sixteen

The astonishing thing to Rafe was that three little humans could come out of his beautiful wife. He couldn't believe his eyes as one, two, three daughters were taken from his wife's stomach in an emergency cesarean procedure.

He wasn't allowed to do much. He could watch, and comfort Julie. The babies were born early enough to still be considered high risk, so they were whisked away.

But they were healthy, and viable, and Rafe thanked God for that. "You're amazing," he told his wife.

She didn't say anything. He reached for her hand, heartened that she seemed to accept his fingers holding hers. Her skin was so cold it scared him. "I think she's cold," he told the delivering doctor and anesthesiologist and the army of nurses doing their jobs.

He himself felt warm as toast. Too warm, in fact.

"We're taking good care of her, Mr. Callahan," he was advised, and Rafe focused on holding Julie's hand. He'd never felt so helpless in his life.

What could he do for her?

Did she even want his help? She'd called him to take her to the doctor, and then the hospital, so he tried to take comfort from that. But it was hard when she'd been distant since around Christmas.

Maybe now that their daughters were born, everything would be different. He prayed so.

"Hey, gorgeous," he said softly, "how are you feeling?"

Julie didn't answer. She turned to look at him, her steady gaze melting him. Then she closed her big brown eyes in exhaustion.

Rafe reminded himself to not ask any more stupid questions.

WHEN JULIE AWAKENED THE next day, her life went into overdrive. The nurses wanted her to try to express breast milk. This was harder than it sounded, because she was sore from the stitches in her abdomen, and more tired than she'd ever been. Rafe left the room in a hurry every time nurses came in after that, the breast milk thing obviously throwing him for a loop.

She worried constantly about the babies. "They weren't supposed to come so early," she told a nurse.

"Happy Valentine's Day," the nurse responded cheerfully. "There are roses outside your door, which are about to be delivered. Your husband's quite the romantic."

"I know." Julie wrinkled her nose. She didn't want roses from Rafe. At the moment, she didn't know what she wanted, but it wasn't romance.

"He keeps going down to the nursery and staring at them. And asking what their names are." The nurse smiled. "He doesn't like that their bassinets say Jenkins/Callahan #1, #2, #3."

Julie shook her head. "We haven't discussed names."

The nurse looked at her. "You have a lactation consultant coming this afternoon to help you learn some techniques for breast-feeding triplets. And do you want a baby name book?"

"No, thank you." Julie was too tired to think about names

right now. She felt guilty about it, but Rafe was the father. He deserved some share in the naming of their daughters.

The fact that she'd kept him away from her for the past six weeks had postponed the discussion. Or debate, as the case usually went. "I gained sixty pounds," she told the nurse.

The small, dark-haired woman laughed. "Count yourself lucky."

"He keeps calling me gorgeous. I don't feel gorgeous. I feel enormous."

"Don't burst his bubble." The nurse left the room, and Rafe arrived just as the flowers were being carried in.

Three bouquets of lovely pink roses. Julie looked at him. "This wasn't necessary."

Rafe pulled a chair close to her bed. "It was. And I've been snapping photos of our daughters. They look a little scary right now, very extraterrestrial, with all the tubes and stuff. But they look healthy to me." He smiled, his face tired. "Can I get you anything?"

"No, thanks." Julie sneaked a look at him, wondering how the most handsome, rugged man in Diablo had ended up at her bedside, when she was the most rumpled, overweight woman in town. "Perhaps a new body."

He patted her hand. "I bet you'll feel better in a few months. It probably takes a while for everything to acclimatize."

Julie sniffed. "I guess so. Rafe, listen. I want to apologize for—"

He squeezed her fingers, then kissed them. "Don't apologize for anything. Just rest."

"But I want you to know that you can see your daughters whenever you like. I shouldn't have kicked you out before." Julie looked at her hand, which was held in Rafe's. She'd missed him so much. "The whole situation has been so confusing."

"It doesn't matter. We have our daughters, and that's going to be our focus from now on."

Julie didn't know what to say. He didn't really understand that with the birth of the babies, the divorce could be filed anytime. The small connection holding them together was over.

"You're thinking too hard, Judge," Rafe said. "I'm ordering you to rest. Or name your daughters. One or the other, but stop sitting there borrowing trouble. I can feel the vibes."

Julie looked at him. "Naming is your job."

He shook his head. "Nope. I want no part of it. Whatever I pick they'll hate later on, and blame it on me."

Julie smiled. "So you want me to be the bad guy?"

"You have more experience with what girls like," he said.

"I wouldn't necessarily agree," Julie said, glancing around at the beautiful roses in her room. "I'll do first names, you do middle names."

"I'll try." He sounded doubtful. "I don't even name the horses at our ranch."

"Well, this time you can't pass the buck." Julie thought about her mother, and said, "Janet."

"I like that." Rafe looked at her. "Let's see. We have, in order of appearance, Fiona, Molly and Elizabeth. Those are Jackie and Pete's. Then we have Joy Patrice, who is Creed and Aberdeen's little one, and the new one she's expecting around the middle of March. Creed hits singles," Rafe said, bragging just a touch. "That baby will be named Grace Marie, according to Aberdeen. Of course, we must count in Aberdeen's sister Diane's young'uns, who live at the ranch, which are Ashley, Suzanne and Lincoln Rose." Rafe squinted. "And Judah and Darla's are Jennifer Belle and Molly Mavis. That last one is named for my mother, and then Darla's mother is Mavis Night. Mavis had Darla very late in life—almost a miracle, she always said. Unlike

Corinne, whose daughter was born much earlier. She married early, and moved up north. Corinne was enjoying having her nieces, Seton and Sabrina, around, not that she got to see them much because they were always helping out at your place." Rafe puzzled over all the names he'd mentioned, looking at Julie. "That's a lot of females in our town, isn't it?"

The mention of Seton and Sabrina had put a scowl on her face. In fact, all the names he'd just thrown out annoyed Julie. It was typical in the small town of Diablo to know everybody's business and think of everyone as family, but she didn't like it.

In fact, she was jealous. She frowned, looking at her big husband. She was so jealous she wanted to crab all over Rafe, who was staring at her innocently, unaware that he'd just stirred up a cauldron of anxiety inside her.

She wasn't supposed to be jealous. She was supposed to be mad at him for hiring plants. Not that he'd done it himself, but he'd probably been aware of his aunt's perfidy. Julie pressed her lips together. "Now that you've gone through the roll call, did you think of anything?"

"I'm working on it," he said. "I don't think as quickly as you do."

"If I'd been thinking quickly, I would never have allowed you to—"

Rafe blinked as she cut off her words. "Allowed me to what?"

She shook her head. "Don't mind me. All kinds of toads are trying to fly out of my mouth today."

"You're angry with me." Rafe nodded. "I can understand that. But, Julie, they're beautiful little girls. We can't let bitterness color our lives with them in it."

"I know." Julie was ashamed. "I'm sorry. I've been having a lot of negative thoughts lately."

"Go ahead. Spill to Rafe. I'm the thinker of the family, you know."

She rolled her eyes. "I'm not proud of the way I've been thinking. I'm jealous."

"Of what?"

She wasn't going to feed his ego by telling him that she didn't really want the divorce, when she knew he did. It was a practical solution for two people who would never have gotten together if not for a pregnancy. "I've gained so much weight I couldn't wear the magic wedding dress that the other Callahan brides wore."

Rafe looked shocked. "Julie Jenkins Callahan, that doesn't sound like you at all."

She sank against her pillow. "I know. And yet I am jealous. We didn't get married at the ranch, either, like the other brides."

"Holy smokes," Rafe said. "Is that what's been bugging you?"

"Among a few other things," Julie admitted.

"Well, we don't live at Rancho Diablo like everyone else does, either," Rafe pointed out. "You bought a house in town. Is that going to bother you, too?"

Julie considered that. She thought about her daughters living so far away from their cousins and aunts and uncles, and nodded, a little embarrassed. "I think it does."

Rafe shook his head. "Let's go back to naming our daughters, shall we?"

Julie looked at him. "All right," she said, her voice small. "Rafe, by the way, this summer I plan on getting back to hearing cases."

He stared at her for a long time. Then he said, "Whatever you think is best," and left the room.

Julie gazed at the roses after he was gone, wishing she was better at saying what she really felt.

"I THINK," SAM SAID, "that what Julie was trying to tell you is that she doesn't feel married to you. She doesn't feel part of the family. So she's going on with her life, making the plans she needs to make."

Rafe had been poleaxed by everything his wife had told him. "I don't even know her."

"That's probably true," Sam said cheerfully. "You'd best get a move on, bro."

"Like I know how." Rafe was honestly perplexed. "I think it's too late."

"Maybe. But you can't fail the Callahans now. All of us have caught our women, and are pretty happy about it."

"You don't have a woman," Rafe said, irritated.

"I was speaking in the familial possessive."

"Whatever," Rafe said.

"My point is, you're going to have to try harder," Sam said. "Truthfully, we don't think you've been giving it your best effort."

"We?"

"The family."

"Ah, yes. The familial plural." Rafe stared at his tiny babies through the glass of the preemie nursery, his heart sick and sore. "I'd do anything for them."

"Of course you would." Sam clapped him on the back. "So marry their mother again."

Rafe's jaw clenched. "That is not the answer."

"Sure it is. What Julie was trying to tell you, dunderhead—though she may not have realized she was saying this—is that she feels like you two got married under the gun. For these babies. And you'd already baked in the divorce. Now she wants to know that you want to marry her for her." Sam looked pleased with himself. "And you're supposed to be the thinker in the family. Ha!"

Sam went off down the hall to see Julie. Rafe turned to

look at his lovely daughters who he thought were tough little nuts, like their mother. They wailed for the nurses, and got their share of attention, and then sometimes they lay quite still, doing their baby thing. He was proud of them, so proud he didn't know what to do. "One of you is named Janet," he whispered, "because Julie loved her mother. And you'll love your mother, because she's special."

He heard a camera click at his elbow. Part of him wasn't surprised to see Chief Running Bear taking a few fast snaps. "Fancy meeting you here," Rafe murmured.

"Not really," Running Bear said. He grinned, looking pleased.

"What's with all the baby photos?" Rafe asked. "I found the pictures under the rock in the cave, so I know you're collecting them."

"Not really." Running Bear snapped a few more, then nodded at Rafe. "You have been blessed. These babies keep your family heritage alive."

"Isn't that what babies do?" Rafe asked.

The chief ignored him. "Six brothers, all girl children. It's a good sign."

"Wait," Rafe said, grabbing the man's arm as he prepared to depart. "A good sign for what?"

"A good life." Running Bear nodded, and when Rafe released him, went silently down the hall.

Rafe looked back at his daughters. "All right, good signs," he said. "Good sign number one, you're Janet. Good sign number two, your name is Julianne. And good sign number three, your name is Judith, because three *J*'s will likely really drive your mom nuts, and because it's a jackpot. Three *J*'s in a row." He wished he could kiss their small fuzzy heads, but that wouldn't be allowed for weeks. "I have to go explain to your mother now why I picked the first names and she's going to have to do the middle names. I deviated from my assignment."

Rafe walked into his wife's room, astonished to find Bode sitting by her bed. "Jenkins," he said, not happy to see his father-in-law.

"Callahan," Bode growled.

"Not now, you two," Julie said.

"I'll go," Rafe said.

"You do that," Bode said.

Julie clapped her hands to demand their attention. "There is going to be order in my family whether either of you like it or not. This ceases today." Her eyes flashed at both of them. "Family dinners are not going to be things of misery. Family occasions are not going to be had with each of you in a separate corner. So shake right now."

They ignored her.

"Shake," Julie said, "or I'll kick both of you out and nobody will be holding any babies."

Rafe and Bode shook hands in the fastest timing Rafe could manage. They glared at each other, although Rafe tried to temper his glare slightly for Julie's sake.

"I'm going," Bode stated. To Rafe he said, "You do anything to upset my daughter, and I'll—"

"You'll do nothing," Rafe snapped. "That's for damn sure."

Bode left. Julie burst into tears.

"Cripes," Rafe said, sinking onto the chair next to her bed. He was still steaming. "Don't cry, Julie. It's going to take some time for our family to connect." It would take a hundred years, but he wasn't going to say that to her. Right now, she might take his head off.

"Hey," he said, trying to curry favor with his wife, "I named the babies. Janet, Julianne and Judith—*J*'s all the way across. Jackpot."

Julie pointed to the door. "Out."

His heart dropped. "Why? What did I say?"

"Rafe Callahan, this has been nothing but a game for you, nothing but a gamble. You wanted me off your family's court case in the beginning, and—"

"*My* family's court case?" Rafe interrupted. "Your father sued *us*." He didn't want to think about Sam's plan. "And the whole thing was dumb, anyway, because we don't own the mineral rights to Rancho Diablo."

She stopped crying, staring at him over her tissue. "What?"

He shrugged. "We don't."

"Who does?"

"A Navajo chief. His tribe, actually." Rafe looked at her. "What your father wants with more land is beyond me. He's five years behind paying the taxes on his own land."

Her jaw dropped. "Get out. Get out. Get out!"

Rafe jumped up. "Julie, we have to put this behind us once and for all, if we're ever going to be a family. You have to know the truth—"

She pointed at the door. Rafe's shoulders drooped and he slunk out.

In the hall, Jonas waved a bouquet of flowers at him.

"I just heard the sound of a marriage blowing up," his brother said. "And right after Valentine's Day, too." He shook his head. "Are you sure you're the smart one in the family?"

Jonas went into Julie's room, which Rafe thought was brave, considering she probably didn't want to see any Callahans at the moment.

She certainly didn't want to see him.

Utterly deflated, Rafe headed home.

Chapter Seventeen

"I don't know what happened," Rafe told his sister-in-law Jackie. He was paying a call on her at the bridal shop she co-owned with Darla. It was a handy thing to have two sisters-in-law in the bridal business, he decided. "It's like my mouth left my face and started quacking. I think it was seeing Bode. The shock of him sitting there just got me angry."

Jackie nodded. "I understand. But you're going to have to put Julie first. Being a mom of triplets is hard, Rafe. Everything is times three. Take it from me."

"You and Pete seemed to take everything in stride."

"Trust me, there were times I told him to go put his head in the horses' trough." Jackie shook her head. "You guys just saw the happy side. We kept the darker days to ourselves." She smiled at him. "In six months, everything is going to look different, Rafe. Don't give up hope."

"Six months!" He didn't think he could wait that long for things to straighten out for him and Julie. "Isn't there a shortcut?"

Jackie laughed. "I don't think so. Not from where you two are starting. Anyway, babies tend to put relationships in a different gear."

"It seems I've been waiting forever," Rafe said. He felt as if hope was sifting away for him and Julie.

"And you love her," Jackie said.

"And I love her," Rafe repeated. He looked at his sister-in-law, who was smiling at him. "I really do."

"I know you do." She handed him a box of hand-me-down baby clothes. "Give these to Julie, please, and see if she can use them. I found that what my babies used the most were little nighties and onesies in the beginning."

"Thanks. Hey, Jackie?"

"Yes?" She smiled at him.

"Do you know whatever happened to that magic wedding gown thing? It wouldn't still be at your shop, would it?" He was hoping the darn thing hadn't gone with Sabrina when she'd left town. Julie had seemed really interested in wearing the gown, which had shocked him.

"It's here." Jackie's brows rose. "You're not needing it, are you?"

"I'm not sure. Can I see it?" Rafe asked on a whim.

She went into the back, bringing out a heavy clear sack encasing a long, beautiful white gown. He could see sequins and beads and all kinds of sparkly things on the fabric.

"Very different from what we had to fit her in for her wedding," Jackie said with a laugh. "Most of the Callahan brides managed to get into the dress before we got too huge to fit."

"Yeah." Rafe looked at the dress through the bag, trying to decide why it would matter to Julie. "Isn't a dress a dress, though?"

Jackie smiled. "Not to a woman."

"I guess." He didn't think Julie could have been more beautiful than the day he'd married her. "She doesn't seem like she'd be the sentimental type, though. Rather, all-business and judgelike."

"She feels like she's outside the family circle." Jackie hung the dress on a hook at the wrap stand. "You can take it with you if you like."

She went off to help some customers who walked in. Rafe looked at the gown for a while, thinking he might not ever understand women.

Then he grabbed the dress and headed out.

For Julie, he'd do anything.

AT THE END OF MARCH, Rafe and Julie were finally allowed to take the triplets home. Julie let him help her with the three car seats, let him drive them home, let him carry the babies upstairs. He was proud to see that the names he'd selected had been painted over each daughter's crib.

He was pretty certain Julie would want him to leave. Things were so awkward and uncomfortable between them. She looked stronger, she looked beautiful—if a little tired—and the last thing he wanted to do was upset her.

So he went to the front door. "If there's anything you need, feel free to call, Julie."

She looked at him, surprised. "Where are you going?"

"Home?"

"Oh." She looked down for a moment. Then she took a deep breath. "I do want you to be part of our girls' lives, Rafe."

"I want that, too," he said quickly, thinking nothing had been right or easy between them since the babies had been born on Valentine's Day.

"This house is big enough for both of us," Julie said.

He looked at the babies in their carriers, still soothed by the car ride home. "You're going to need lots of help, I'm sure."

She didn't say anything. Rafe swallowed, trying again. "I'm happy to stay and help if you want me to."

"If that's what you want." Her chin lifted. "But only if it's what you want."

"It sounds like a good idea to me." Rafe wasn't sure what

more he should be saying or doing. He felt like a fish on the end of a line, dangling. "Just tell me what *you* want." *Because all I want is you.*

She shrugged. "Let's take it a step at a time."

He nodded. Baby steps were fine with him.

JULIE AND RAFE BEGAN a merry-go-round of diapers and feeding and burping and soothing crying infants. He suffered more than Julie did, because she was patient. His daughters' wailing unnerved him, because in his world, if something cried, that was bad, and it needed to be fixed. Half the time he couldn't fix what the problem was—only Julie could. And then there was the random occasion when even Julie couldn't fix the problem. On those nights, he would take whatever daughter was expressing her opinions, and put her on his chest, rocking her until she felt comforted.

"The doctor said it might be gas," Julie stated, and while Rafe was pretty certain that anything as beautiful as his daughters could not possibly have gas, he still encouraged them to toot, and praised them when they did.

"Do you think that's normal parenting?" Julie asked him.

"Ladies are self-conscious about breaking wind," Rafe said. "I want mine to know that the family that breaks wind together, stays together."

Julie winced and went back upstairs. "Well, it's true," Rafe told Julianne. "You just send that gas right out the back of your little diaper. Daddy's got a catcher's mitt, sweetie."

He spent a lot of time rocking his daughters. In fact, he spent so much time doing it that he ordered an extra rocker, this one with a cushioned back and arms. "Now this is a chair," he told Julie, when she came down to look at it. "I had to move your flowered pincushion into the dining room, though."

Julie glanced at the ottoman she'd loved, and went back upstairs.

"We exist on two levels," Rafe told Sam, who was visiting. "She's mostly upstairs, me mostly downstairs. I have a big-screen TV, though, so it's working for us."

"Congratulations, I guess." Sam looked at him. "Which baby is this?"

"This pink-faced doll is Judith." Rafe grinned. "She tends to be the noisiest because she was born last. She thinks she has to stand up for herself, so she's the squeakiest wheel."

"You know," Sam said, "perhaps the reason the two of you exist on two levels is because Julie's figured out that you're a bit odd."

"Nah," Rafe said. "I'm the only normal one in the family."

"Which family?" Sam asked.

"The Callahan family." Rafe looked surprised. "Why are you asking that dumb question? Julie and these babies are all Callahans. Unless you've heard differently."

"No," Sam said hurriedly.

Rafe looked at his brother. "Tell me before I wring your neck. I've been lifting babies for a couple of weeks and am therefore packing extra muscle. And, I might add, am a little edgy from lack of sleep."

"Sheesh," Sam said. "It's just that you might want to know that I filed a motion for countersuit today."

"Great," Rafe said. "That ought to put the finishing touches on my failing marriage. The nuclear option usually wipes out everything in its path, doesn't it?"

"Think of the future, Rafe. We have a ton of children at Rancho Diablo now to consider. You don't want the ranch taken away from your daughters, do you? This is the way to stop Bode."

It was also a fast way to stop Julie from thinking of him as a husband. Yet it couldn't be helped. "Judith, if I give you to Uncle Sam here, would you please spit up on him for Daddy?"

Sam hopped up. "I'd go upstairs to say hi to Julie, but perhaps today is not the best time."

"I'm pretty sure you're right." Rafe didn't know what he was going to do about his wife. He was no closer to being with her than he had been. Hell, he was no closer to being a husband than he'd ever been. "Sam, listen, I need you to do me a favor."

"Anything," Sam said, but when Rafe told him what he wanted, his brother's face went white as a sheet.

JULIE LOVED HER DAUGHTERS. She would never have imagined she could love anything as much as she did them. Except Rafe. She shouldn't love him, maybe, but she did, even though it hurt her father. There was a lot of pain on both sides. Although she'd almost relented and asked Nadine, Corinne and Mavis to help a couple of hours every day, she wanted Rafe to have time with his daughters.

First, he began by helping her at night.

Then she noticed some of his clothes were hanging in a guest room closet. His shampoo, toothbrush, et cetera, showed up in the adjoining bath.

This all seemed reasonable to her. There were times when neither of them got more than an hour of sleep at a time. Grabbing a shower whenever possible was paramount.

He slept downstairs on the sofa. This made sense, because if either of them could catch some sleep, it was best to do it. Never did they both sleep at the same time, even with the Books'n'Bingo Society's help.

Julie learned to nurse double football style—and Rafe learned that she wanted privacy during that time. It was too embarrassing, feeling as if she was exposed completely—

which she was. There was simply no delicate way to feed two infants at the same time.

Although Rafe said it was probably the most beautiful thing a man could ever see, he would dutifully take whichever baby wasn't nursing, and go downstairs with her and a bottle. At night, he brought Julie dinner that someone made, or takeout.

He said he'd given up cooking at the ranch starting on Valentine's Day, the babies' birthday. Apparently, Sam and Jonas were eating a lot of Rice Krispies and takeout from Banger's Bait and Tackle.

Julie had just put the babies down and was ready to try to nap herself when she heard Rafe on the stairs. She sat up and tried to look not exhausted.

"Can I come in?" he asked.

She frowned.

Husbands didn't usually have to ask. She hadn't realized there were such clearly defined lines in their living situation. "Of course."

He peeked around the corner. "Everybody decent?"

"Yes." Julie gazed at him. "Just us girls in our gowns."

He didn't look directly at her. "Nadine's here. She's wondering whether, if we take all three babies downstairs, you might be able to nap more than fifteen minutes. She says we can bottle-feed them."

Julie nodded. "That would be wonderful."

"Uh…" He looked at her directly this time. "Corinne is also downstairs. She's wondering if it's all right if she helps."

"I already told her she was welcome anytime." Julie felt bad that she'd asked the three elderly ladies to stop coming by several months ago. Corinne had known nothing of her nieces' employment by Fiona. "Why is she asking?"

"She's just making certain you don't mind her helping out." Rafe looked sheepish. "She wants to do the right thing."

"I'd love to have her." Julie smiled at Rafe. "If the babies are going to be in such good hands downstairs, maybe you should come upstairs and take a nap, too."

He rubbed at his face. "I might sneak into my room and grab a couple of winks. I'm not as tired as you are, but I definitely feel like..." He looked at Julie. She raised her eyebrows and waited.

Rafe hesitated. "You were saying I should nap, too?"

"Mmm-hmm." She patted the bed next to her.

"Oh." He gave her a careful stare. "Are you sure?"

"Absolutely."

After a moment, Rafe grabbed Judith up, carrying her downstairs with almost indecent speed. Julie jumped from the bed quickly and ran into her bathroom to swish mouthwash and splash her face, brush her hair.

When Rafe came back, she was back in bed, waiting.

"I don't know if this is a good idea," he said. "You need sleep, and I—"

She patted the mattress again.

"Well, never let it be said that a woman had to ask me twice to get into her bed. A wife's wish is her husband's command," Rafe said, diving in beside her.

The bed squeaked under his weight.

"Shh," Julie said, laughing. "The ladies are going to think my bed is possessed."

Rafe sprawled on the pillow next to hers. "I can do an excellent impression of a haunting if given the chance."

"Today, just a nap," Julie said. "Hold me, cowboy, if you want to."

Rafe wrapped his arms around her, and Julie fell asleep, feeling as if she'd finally made a wise decision.

FIVE HOURS LATER Julie woke up. Rafe was long gone, because "his" side of the bed was cold. She smiled to herself. The most wonderful feeling had stolen over her as they'd slept in each other's arms.

For the first time, she began to believe that their marriage might survive.

She wanted that, she realized, more than anything.

After a fast shower, she went downstairs. Rafe was alone, the ladies gone.

"Why didn't you wake me up?" Julie asked.

He shrugged from the recliner. "They're asleep. No need to wake Mom unless the princesses are demanding dinner. How did you sleep?"

"Like a baby." Julie smiled at him, then surprised both him and herself by crawling up into his lap and resting her head on his shoulder. "I never did thank you for everything you did while I was bed-bound."

"I didn't do much." He rubbed her back, his hand moving in slow circles across her shoulders. It felt so wonderful to be in his arms.

"You arranged a wedding. You decorated the nursery."

"I didn't do it all. The ladies did a lot of that. I merely instructed on function. And wrote checks."

Julie smiled. "You picked out baby names."

"That was the hard part. Imagine choosing things you know your daughters are going to complain about."

"They won't." Julie looked at the babies sleeping in the playpen they used as a makeshift downstairs crib, and smiled. "The doctor says they're growing fast. And that given time, maybe all the little kinks will lessen."

"Soccer will help the lungs develop," Rafe said, his voice sleepy. "Riding horses will develop strong bodies."

Julie smiled. "Is that what happened to you?"

"Not so much. Fiona gave us all the ranch chores to do." Rafe laughed softly. "That grows a boy into a man quick.

But my little angels aren't going to be allowed to do ranch chores."

"They have to," Julie said. "Otherwise, they won't be independent."

He nuzzled her neck. "How did *you* get so independent?"

Julie opened her mouth to say she'd always been that way. Losing her mother at a young age had forced her to stand on her own two feet. "I don't know that I am, anymore. I've become pretty dependent on you."

"That'll change when you go back to being a judge."

Julie thought for a moment about what she wanted Rafe to know. "What I meant was, I've come to a place where I really enjoy being with you."

He turned her chin so that he could look into her eyes. "I enjoy being with you, too."

"I'd like our marriage to work, Rafe. If that's what you want," Julie said, her heart practically in her hands.

He kissed her on the lips. "It is what I want. I was hoping you'd decide to keep me at some point."

"Let's keep it open a little while longer," Julie said, thinking that things had been going almost too smoothly in the past few weeks. "I feel like good things are happening. But I'm still afraid."

He ran a hand down her shoulder-length dark hair. "Don't be afraid of me, sweetheart. I'm easy."

She was afraid, because it was so hard to blend their families. "I'm glad you're here," she said softly, and Rafe brushed a soft kiss against her lips.

"I'm not going anywhere, unless you say so."

They sat like that, holding each other, for a long time, until their daughters woke up. But even when they had to let each other go, Julie could have sworn she could still feel

Rafe touching her, stroking her skin, making her feel he loved her.

Hope began to build inside her heart.

Chapter Eighteen

Rafe was pretty certain his wife's change of heart where he was concerned was due to the babies. He wasn't complaining.

He sat in the barn, staring at Bleu, who seemed interested in chatting with him today. "Life is good," he told the big horse. "It's all going to work out."

He had a lot of plans.

Jonas came into the barn, putting a few bridles he'd repaired on their hooks. "Still talking to yourself? We've noticed you do that a lot."

"It's all right," Rafe said. "I'm damn good company."

Jonas laughed. "Did you hear Creed's baby was born last night?"

Rafe sat up. "No. How is Aberdeen? Did everything go all right?"

"Everything's fine. Creed's bragging that Aberdeen gave birth naturally. I guess he's hoping that'll mean his baby is getting the best possible start in life."

Rafe grinned. "That's awesome. I'll have to go by the hospital."

"How's your crowd?"

Rafe's grin stretched wider. "We're all fine."

"We?" His brother looked at him. "You're part of the family now?"

"It's looking better." Rafe had a lot of hope for himself and Julie. He was positive that they belonged together forever. There just couldn't be any other way. Certainly no woman was made for him like Julie was. He adored her, from her delicate toes to her mass of midnight hair. "We're getting the hang of things."

"That's good to hear." Jonas shrugged. "Since you reneged on your chef duties, Sam and I have reshuffled things a bit."

"I guess you two are batching these days, huh?" Rafe asked, not feeling sorry for his brothers at all. "I guess you could always try to find a woman who might have you."

"Nope." Jonas shook his head. "I see what you and all my brothers are going through, and I get real content with my bachelorhood. You guys are not exactly poster dads for married life."

"You're jealous." Rafe grinned. "Anyway, try it, you might like it."

"No, Fiona's hex will pass me by. Thanks."

"It wasn't a hex, it was a blessing."

Jonas laughed. "Whatever. I'll believe that when Julie decides to keep you." He left, whistling a tune from *Seven Brides for Seven Brothers.*

Rafe thought his eldest brother might possibly be annoying in a league of his own. "Sourpuss," he muttered. Of course Julie was going to keep him. And he was most definitely going to keep Julie.

It was too beautiful a May morning to pay attention to his brother's dark moods. Rafe decided to ride Bleu to clear his head.

Jonas had made him nervous. He'd go home and find his wife, and he'd tell her. He'd tell her that he loved her, and how much she meant to him, and surely everything would start coming together.

WHEN RAFE WALKED INTO the house that night, it was dark. He didn't hear the sounds of babies crying, or Julie singing, or the Books'n'Bingo Society ladies chattering. It was strange.

"Julie?" he called. "I'm home."

She came down the stairs, pale as a ghost.

"What's wrong?" he asked. "Are you all right?"

"First," Julie said, "I want you to take this stupid chair off the rail."

"Okay," Rafe said. "That can be easily done." He watched his wife carefully. Now that she came closer to him, Rafe realized she looked angry, really angry. "What happened?"

"You happened," Julie said, her voice tight. "Your family happened."

He hesitated, his heart sinking. "Tell me what's going on. All I know is that Aberdeen and Creed had their baby today, baby Grace Marie. A whopping seven-pounder with blue eyes, her mom's chocolate-brown hair and her dad's full set of lungs."

That seemed to stop her for a moment, but then Julie speared him with another deliberate look. "My father got the papers today."

"What papers?" Rafe felt his heart rate jack up. If Bode was involved in whatever had upset Julie, things did not look bright for the home team.

"The countersuit. Your family suing my father for his ranch. I remember you saying something about my dad owing five years of back taxes." Julie crossed her arms. "Too good an opportunity to pass up, was it?"

Rafe shook his head. "Don't talk to me about any of that. I didn't know the papers were actually filed."

"But you knew they would be. You knew it was your brother's plan." Her eyes blazed. "You're a scoundrel, Rafe Callahan."

"Julie." Rafe rubbed the back of his neck. "The legal thing

is going to drag on for years, as long as your father wants it to. You can't keep getting all ginned up every time there's a twist or turn in the proceedings."

"As long as my father wants it to?"

Rafe nodded. "Well, hell, yeah. You wouldn't expect us not to defend ourselves, would you? And while we're on the topic, may I remind you that you're a Callahan now. Those are Callahan children, Julie. Whether you accept it or not, you're playing for Team Callahan. You need to think about your daughters' futures." He shrugged. "You're my wife."

"I'm my father's daughter."

"But this is your family now. I'm your family, and the girls are your family. I don't really see a conflict."

"The conflict," Julie said, her tone furious, "is that you just can't leave my father alone. You're not going to leave him with any pride."

Rafe shrugged again. "If that's the cost of getting him out of our hair, so be it. His pride is little concern to me. I'm not playing for pride, Julie. I'm playing for my family. Of which you are the most important part."

She turned away. "I don't know what to say to you, Rafe."

"Where are the babies?"

"At my father's." Julie turned back around. "I'm going home."

"The hell you are." Rafe frowned at her. "Julie Callahan, you go get my children right now and bring them back here where they belong. I don't know what poison your father's whispered in your ear, and I don't care. But you and my daughters are going to stay right here in this house that you bought, because you wanted to be free of your father. And quit wearing me out with this mean-to-Daddy routine. Somebody needs to straighten that old cuss out. It's unfortunate that it has to be us, but we'll do it."

"I know you will," Julie snapped, "and that's the problem."

"Would you prefer if we rolled over?"

She didn't answer.

Rafe looked at her for a long time. "All right, Julie," he said softly, "you win. You go get my daughters, and you bring them back here where all their things are. I'll go. And I won't be back." He took a deep breath. "I concede that you were right all along. Next month is June, a perfect month for a divorce. So file."

He left, his heart shredded to ribbons.

But there really wasn't anything he could do. Julie had made her decision long ago.

JULIE WAS ASTONISHED when Rafe walked out. She wanted so much to think she'd made the right decision. After her father's visit, when he'd told her about the countersuit, she'd realized Rafe had been keeping things from her once again. Important things. And she'd known then that, in his mind, she was very separate from whatever happened at the Callahans' ranch. Whatever they were going to do to her father, he would never share with her. This was the second time he hadn't warned her of what was coming.

It was almost as if she existed on the periphery of his mind. Love could not exist unless both partners shared everything.

And he'd walked out. She'd wanted to go away for a few days to her father's, keep an eye on him. She was really afraid he was going to have a heart attack or a stroke with this latest ploy by the Callahans.

She felt so torn, so caught in the middle.

But she'd never expected Rafe to just leave. It seemed as if he'd given up, almost as if he'd known he would. Planned it.

They'd agreed to stay together until after the babies were born. And he'd kept to that part of the bargain.

Julie wondered how long he'd known that there was going to be this dastardly countersuit. It really was a trick to beat all tricks.

The Callahans were, as her dad had always said, capable of anything.

Cold fear stole over her. She was worried for her father.

Yet she was absolutely terrified her marriage was over.

And she didn't see any way to put trust back between her and Rafe. Maybe because it had never existed at all.

TWO DAYS LATER, Sam and Jonas looked at their brother as he sat perched on a fence rail, staring out onto Julie's father's land.

"Wanna grab some grub?" Jonas asked him.

"I don't feel like eating. Thanks." His wife and daughters were in that house, having "gone home," as Julie put it. He missed them. He supposed he'd miss them a lot more in the coming years.

Sam cleared his throat. "You've been up there all morning. You can't stay there all day."

Rafe shrugged. "I'll come in eventually."

Jonas sighed. "Why don't you just go ring the doorbell and ask to see your babies? Julie won't keep them from you."

That wasn't possible. Bode wasn't going to want him showing up to stick his finger in his eye. That's how the old man would feel—and Rafe couldn't blame him.

There was really nothing he could do.

"Nah," Rafe said. "Sometimes it's best to let sleeping dogs lie very still in their own corner."

"You know it had to be done." Sam's voice carried conviction. "There was no other way to stop him."

"You're the family legal beagle. You're heading up

the team of lawyers that's going to save this ranch." Rafe shrugged. "I'm fully confident that you're the only man who can do it. So whatever happens, happens."

Jonas leaned his elbows on the wood rail. "Did you tell her you didn't know when it was getting filed?"

He shook his head. "It wouldn't have mattered. It's still *Callahans* v. *Jenkins*. It always will be."

"Look," Sam said, pointing.

Rafe turned toward the south. And there, highlighted by the dusky canyons, the black Diablo mustangs ran, hooves flying and manes straight out like flags. The hair rose on Rafe's arms. Besides his daughters, the Diablos were the most beautiful things he could ever imagine seeing on this earth. "I'll never cease to be amazed by those mustangs."

His brothers shook their heads. Behind him, Bleu nickered, recognizing kindred spirits at play. They all watched for another five minutes until the dust dissipated and the thunder of hooves could no longer be heard. Then Rafe got down from the rail, and without another look back at the house where his wife and daughters were, he rode to the barn and unsaddled Bleu.

"You want to run with those Diablos," he said to Bleu. "I want my daughters and wife back. We don't always get what we want, old friend."

Bleu snorted. Rafe patted the animal's neck and handed him over to a groom.

They'd always believed—probably because Fiona had told them—that the Diablos running was a mystical portent of things to come. A magical, unexplainable hand of future over Rancho Diablo. The Diablos were one with the land, and the spirits that had guided them there.

Rafe wasn't certain if he still believed his aunt's fairy tales anymore.

Chapter Nineteen

Julie was in the kitchen warming milk for the babies when she heard thunder. "Rain," she murmured. "Your first rain, babies." She'd decided to begin utilizing soy formula and weaning the babies off nursing. They were getting bigger and stronger faster than she'd expected, and the doctor seemed pleased—surprised, even—by their progress. "It's your father's DNA," she murmured, picking up little Janet. "All those brawny Callahan genes are going to help you catch up fast."

She'd just settled in when the doorbell rang. Since her father was upstairs, Julie called, "Come in!"

Her eyes went wide when Seton McKinley walked into the house. "Seton!"

The blonde P.I. smiled. "Am I catching you at a bad time?"

Julie wasn't certain. She should be mad at Seton, shouldn't she? Yet she'd had a lot of time to think. Seton had been good to Bode, and to Julie. Rafe had said that Seton and Sabrina hadn't shared anything about their family after Fiona had left. Didn't that mean Seton was honorable?

Still, she looked at her old friend cautiously. "It's not a bad time. What are you doing back in town?"

Seton looked at her. "I never apologized to you, Julie. I feel I owe you and your father an apology."

"You don't," Julie said quickly. "I don't want an apology."

"I need to offer you one. I should've quit as soon as Fiona left. Instead, I stayed on." Seton smiled at her, then at the baby. "I got too close to your family, I'm afraid."

"Thank you," Julie murmured. "We enjoyed you being with us."

"I hope you can forgive me, Julie."

"It's in the past," she said quickly.

"Thank you. That means a lot to me."

"So," Julie said, not knowing where to take the conversation next. Little Janet was busy taking her bottle, completely unworried about her mother's tenseness. "What are you doing now?"

"I've been working in D.C. But I'm planning to stay here this summer with Aunt Corinne." Seton walked to the door, about to depart. "It's good to see you again, Julie. You look well. Tell your father I said hello."

"Wait." Julie cleared her throat. "I'm certain that this is confidential. I'm aware that what you do is client sensitive. But I have to know something. Did you ever report anything to Rafe? Did he ever ask you anything about our family?"

Seton shook her head. "The brothers weren't really aware of what was going on. Fiona and Burke were in charge at the time. I understand everything's changed now."

Julie's brow wrinkled. Janet had finished drinking, so she put her to her shoulder to work out a burp. "What's changed?"

"Sam's heading most everything now, along with Jonas. I think they're making joint decisions. The other brothers are too busy with their families. At least that's what I heard from Aunt Corinne."

Julie frowned. "What about Rafe?"

"Rafe doesn't do anything except work."

"What does that mean?" Julie felt a strange tickling sensation in her conscience.

"According to my aunt, he's not involved in ranch decisions."

Julie blinked. "I don't understand."

Seton shrugged. "I'm sure it's complicated. Goodbye, Julie. It was nice seeing you."

"Good to see you, too," she said. "Will you mind if I don't walk you to the door?"

"I know my way." Seton left, and Julie sank back in the chair, rubbing little Janet's back.

How could Rafe not be involved in ranch decisions? All the brothers shared everything equally. Fiona's big idea of giving the ranch to the brother with the largest family had started things off with a bang. But if Rafe had known all along that he'd be asking for a divorce, that would make him ineligible, according to Fiona's rules.

Had he not cared? "Maybe it didn't matter," she told Janet. "Maybe Fiona changed the rules."

He wouldn't give up his share of the ranch because of Julie. But if he was no longer making executive decisions about the ranch and the running of it, when she knew darn well he'd been "the thinker" and a chief decision maker, something had changed. Drastically.

"I don't understand your father," she told baby Janet. She listened for her other daughters, who were upstairs sleeping, but no sounds filtered to her.

The doorbell rang, startling her. "Come in," Julie called, wondering if Seton had returned.

The door opened and Sam poked his head inside. "I should have called first, I know. But I'm afraid of waking babies. Around the Callahan ranch, a ringing telephone has been known to upset a baby or two. And new moms don't like that."

Julie was astonished. This was the first Callahan who'd ever come to this house, unless she counted the time Rafe had sneaked in through her window. She didn't.

"If my father sees you, it won't be a telephone that upsets the babies," she told Sam.

He grinned. "Brave of me, isn't it?"

"Or crazy." She looked at him. "Seton was just here."

His dark blue eyes went wide. "Seton?"

Julie wondered if Rafe was correct about Sam having a thing for the private investigator. "Just missed her."

"What's she doing in town?"

"Visiting her aunt, I think. What are you doing here?" Julie worked up a glare, but it was hard. Sam was one of her favorite Callahans, if she could bridge family loyalty enough to have a favorite.

"I need you to sign some papers." He held up his briefcase. "Can I come in?"

"Yes." Julie nodded. "But please keep your voice down. I don't want my dad to know you're here."

"Sneaking me in like a thief?" Sam grinned.

"Or a lawyer." Julie looked at him as he dug around in his briefcase. Her heart suddenly sank. "You've brought divorce papers, haven't you?"

He stared at her. "Divorce papers?"

Julie nodded. She felt tears burn at the back of her eyes, told herself she wasn't about to cry. Not over her marriage.

Yes, she was. As soon as Sam left, she was going to bawl like Janet and Julianne and Judith. Rafe's jackpots. "Arghh," she said, "Rafe told me to file. He got tired of waiting for me to do it, didn't he? So he did it."

"Jeez," Sam said, "I don't do family law. My specialty is property and otherwise. You'll have to ask Rafe about all that."

Julie's breath came back into her lungs with a whoosh.

"Oh." She wanted to say thank heaven, but bit the words back. Sam was already looking at her as if she had two heads. "What do you need me to sign, then?"

He gave her another assessing glance, then spread some papers out on the coffee table. "These documents pertain to Rafe's sixth of the ranch, which will now be held in trust for Janet, Julianne and Judith. They will now be the sole owners, split three ways, of course, of that portion of Rancho Diablo. You and Rafe, naturally, will be executors until the girls are of age." Sam looked carefully at the papers. "Actually, you'll be joint executors until the girls are forty years old. Rafe felt it was a lot of ranch and business for the girls to undertake when they're twenty-one."

Julie stared at Sam. "I don't understand."

"Well," he said, looking at her, "Rafe's sixth of the ranch is his daughters', once you sign these papers."

"Why?" Julie asked, completely confused. She hadn't ever considered the ranch in relation to her daughters. Her father had always wanted Rancho Diablo—but now Rafe was handing his share of it over to her daughters.

Just like that.

"Why would he do that?" she asked, growing more nervous. She was trying to think fast, but her brain seemed slushy. A divorce between them would mean perhaps some of the ranch might be awarded to Julie. Their daughters would receive monthly support. But a full sixth of the property was a lot of wealth.

It was worth millions.

Julie stared at Sam. "What's going on?"

"Rafe recused himself. That's what he said," Sam told her. "He said you'd recused yourself from the case, and so was he. And he instructed me to draw up these papers." Sam shrugged. "He loves those little girls."

"I know." Julie stared at the papers. "But he hates my

father. He's been fighting for years to keep Rancho Diablo away from my family."

Sam waved his hand with a grin. "Bode'll be long gone before the little ladies hit forty. Trust me, Rafe's not stupid." His brother laughed. "Anyway, sign these papers, will you? Before Bode catches me down here? I'm a lawyer. I do my fighting in court, Judge."

"Believe me, I know, Counselor." Julie gave him a wry glare, not altogether pleased that Sam had teased her about Bode passing away. She bit her lip, considering the papers. "I don't know if I want to sign these papers."

She wasn't certain she wanted anything of Rafe's.

Not like this.

"Hey, if we call your father down here, he'll tell you to sign these papers jiffy-quick," Sam said, completely unbothered by the idea.

"I don't need my father to make decisions for me, thank you," Julie retorted.

Sam smiled. "Now, sister-in-law, don't get all irritated. Rafe's doing a good thing for his girls. You should be making that pen fly like lightning."

She wrinkled her nose. "I have to think."

"You won't get more through a divorce," Sam told her, and Julie gasped.

"I don't want more, you ape!" She glared at him. "I don't even want the divorce!"

She clapped a hand over her mouth as Sam smiled at her.

"So that's the way it is, is it?"

Julie looked at him. "Maybe."

He got to his feet, beaming. "Send those papers over to me when you've signed them. Or I can come get them if you send up a smoke signal."

"I'll call you, Counselor, when I've had sufficient time to consider executing these documents."

"Thank you, Your Honor. I'd be real happy to tell my client everything is wrapped up." He bent down to kiss little Janet on her head. "You sweet thing. So good and quiet. I guess the apple does fall far from the tree on occasion, doesn't it?"

"Sam," Julie said, ignoring his teasing, "is Rafe all right?"

Sam looked at her. "He'll be fine."

She nodded. "Thanks."

Sam patted her on the shoulder, then departed.

Julie stared at the front door for a few moments, her head whirling. Then she looked at the documents.

They were dated February 14.

Valentine's Day. The babies' birthday.

Julie blinked. "Oh, Janet," she murmured. "I completely underestimated your father."

Rafe had taken himself out of the picture a long time ago when it came to ranch affairs. He'd put her and the girls first. She'd accused him of plotting against her and her family. No wonder he'd given up.

She had to fix this somehow.

"Somehow," she whispered to her daughter. "Somehow."

It was going to take a miracle.

Chapter Twenty

After a long few moments thinking about everything she'd just learned, Julie took Janet upstairs. "Dad," she said, putting Janet carefully in her portable bassinet and picking up Julianne. "Seton just came by. She said to tell you hello."

"I don't care." Bode glared at her from his chair. "She need not bother coming by to see me."

"She came to apologize." Julie held Julianne to her shoulder, enjoying the feel of her baby. Julianne gave her the strength she needed to do what had to be done.

"She can't be sorry enough for what she did."

"You know, Dad, Seton didn't have to stay here after Fiona left. Seton's apparently a pretty good P.I. She had people lined up to hire her. She stayed here with us because she'd become fond of you."

"I don't care," he said. "A person gets one shot with me. Once I learn I can't trust them, that's it."

Julie shook her head, thinking about Rafe. "It doesn't always work that way, Dad. Sometimes things aren't exactly the way we see them."

"They are from where I sit. My eyesight's fine." He glared at her. "You've let that Callahan make you all wishy-washy. You used to know exactly where your loyalty belonged."

Julie looked at her father. "Dad, listen. Rafe signed over his portion of the ranch to his daughters."

"So?" Bode's brows knitted in a frown. "That doesn't mean anything to me except that he's a sneaky snake. He's just trying to look like a good guy. One-sixth of that ranch is a pittance compared to what I will get."

Julie took a deep breath. "I'm not going to be able to go on with your feud anymore. I've lived it most all of my life. I'm sorry, but as much as I love you, I've got to put my family first."

Bode stared at her. "Don't fall for his tricks, Julie."

She stepped back. "I don't think I am. I know I'm not. Dad, he doesn't want anything from me. He's trying to give me what I never asked for. I don't want their ranch! I never did. Never will." Her eyes filled with tears. "That probably sounds crazy to you. But I don't think I really ever wanted anything but him."

Bode's jaw sagged. "You don't mean that. You can't."

She nodded. "I do. And when I found out I was pregnant, I was happy. I was afraid that what I'd done would hurt you, but I was happy to be pregnant with Rafe's children." Julie wiped her eyes with Julianne's burp cloth. "Dad, try to understand. Rafe is the husband I chose." She kissed Julianne's downy head, then went to kiss her father's cheek. "I love you, Dad. But if you can't accept my decision, and my new life, you should know you probably won't see much of us. I can't go on grieving for Mom with you."

Bode sucked in a breath. He didn't say anything. Julie waited, but he never spoke, and so after a few moments, she left the room.

Then she packed up her daughters. She signed the papers Sam had left, and, her heart free for the first time in years, drove to Rancho Diablo.

RAFE WAS ASTONISHED when the van he'd bought for Julie to transport the babies pulled up in the drive at Rancho Diablo.

He was shocked when she got out and began unloading baby paraphernalia.

He hurried to the van. "Hi, Julie."

"Hello, Rafe." She handed him the signed papers. "I'll get them notarized when I have time. Until then, there you are." She looked at him. "Are you certain you want to give up your ranch?"

He shrugged. "I had to recuse myself, Julie. Same as you did."

She looked into his eyes. "Why?"

"You come first. You and the girls." He looked sad. "It's always going to be that way, no matter what happens between you and me."

"Oh," Julie said. "Rafe, I am so sorry about everything."

"Don't be," he said. "Not everybody gets a happy ending." He poked his head inside the van and looked at the three babies in their car seats. "Except you angels. You get happy endings. Daddy will make certain of that."

They were asleep, so they didn't care about his promise. Rafe didn't mind. Any father would want his daughters to be happy. These were his tiny treasures, Rafe thought. He didn't need the ranch.

"Rafe," Julie said, and he straightened up to face her.

"Yeah?"

She took a deep breath. "Are you going to divorce me?"

His shoulders seemed to slump; his face fell. "If you want me to."

"No, I mean, do you want a divorce?" Julie asked quickly.

"Oh, hell, no. Why would I?" Rafe looked toward his daughters, then back at her. "I never wanted a divorce. It sounded like a good idea at the time, to keep you from panicking. I knew that the pregnancy and then everything else that was happening really bothered you. So I thought it was best to give you the option, so we could get married. But no, I never wanted a divorce."

She nodded. "I don't, either."

He perked up. "You don't?"

"No." Julie shook her head. "In fact, I hope you'll come back home."

"You do?" His expression changed, a smile lighting his face.

"We took a vote," she said, waving a hand to include their daughters. "It was unanimous."

"That's awesome," Rafe said. He kissed her on the lips, then went around to jump in the passenger seat. "How well does this van accelerate?"

Julie laughed and handed him the keys. "Why don't you drive us home, cowboy?"

Rafe smiled at his wife. "Drive the four most beautiful ladies in the state home? That's an offer I can't refuse."

They drove away from Rancho Diablo, and the babies napped in their carriers, comforted by the drive.

"Angels," Rafe said.

"Not always," Julie said, laughing. "But most of the time."

"I have something for you." Rafe helped her carry the babies inside and settle them in their cribs. Then he pulled her to "his" room and opened the closet door.

The magic wedding dress twinkled at Julie. She recognized it immediately. Her gaze shot to Rafe. "Why is this here?"

He shrugged. "You said something about wanting to wear it. And get married at the ranch. And since we had to hurry before—"

Julie squealed and jumped into his arms. "I love you, Rafe Callahan. I'm so happy you're willing to marry me again."

"Well," he said, laughing, "I wasn't sure you'd like the

idea. But I guess that's a yes. And I love you, too, little judge. It's an honor to get to marry you twice."

She kissed him on the lips, overjoyed that he understood how she'd felt. "You don't think it's silly?"

He shook his head. "I think it's smart. A second chance to lock you down? I'd be a fool to pass that up."

"How did you get this dress without me knowing?"

She got down from Rafe's arms and held the wedding gown up to herself, surprised that she felt some kind of electricity run across her skin. It was the stories, of course—romantic nonsense. But she looked at her handsome husband and smiled.

Rafe shrugged. "I told the babies to keep my secret, and they said they would."

Julie held the dress up again. "I can't wait. I felt so frumpy the first time we said I do. I want to be beautiful for you."

"You were beautiful." Rafe winked. "I wanted to undress you and get you into bed as soon as we said I do."

Julie looked at him, then hung the magic wedding dress in the closet. "You know," she said, "while the babies are napping…"

Rafe scooped her into his arms and carried her across the hall to the bed that would now be theirs. "Let the honeymoon begin."

"I remember you boasting that you'd get me in a bed eventually," Julie said, as her husband laid her gently on the sheets. His gaze simmered, promising everything she'd dreamed of.

"I said that," Rafe said, joining his wife in the bed, "and I always keep my promises."

"Although once under the stars and once in my office showed creativity," Julie stated, and Rafe laughed.

"Three's the charm," he said, and proceeded to make love to his wife the way he'd never been able to before, holding her close while the babies slept in their cribs, completely unaware that their parents were now truly husband and wife.

Forever.

Epilogue

Rafe and Julie's wedding day in September was beautiful, with clear blue skies. It was perfect weather for an outdoor wedding—everything Julie had ever hoped for as she prepared to marry the man she loved.

"You're gorgeous," Rafe told her. "I can't wait to get that gown off you, though."

Julie looked down at the magic wedding gown. "This dress is supposed to make certain I know who my perfect husband is. I think it works, too."

Rafe looked devilishly handsome in his black tux. "I don't believe in magic."

She looked at him. "You're the most superstitious man I know."

"All I know is that I'm pretty certain your bikini is going to be more magical than a wedding gown. I'm counting the hours until we get to Tahiti."

"Tahiti!"

Rafe looked at her. "A nice, quiet hut just for the two of us. I don't want any interruptions while I'm alone with my bride."

Julie couldn't wait, either. She'd count the hours until she got her big, strong husband in her arms. "You've thought of everything."

"That's why they call me the thinker." Rafe grinned.

The wedding march began to play. Julie looked at Rafe. "This is it, husband. Speak now or forever hold your peace."

Rafe took her arm to walk her to the altar on Rancho Diablo land. "The only thing I need to say is I love you." He kissed her, and the wedding guests clapped, loving the fact that Rafe clearly intended to romance his wife on the way to the altar.

"I love you, Rafe Callahan. I never thought today would happen, but I'm so glad it is. Thank you." She could feel her eyes twinkling with unshed tears of joy.

"No tears, or your dad'll come after me," Rafe said, glancing toward Bode. "He already looks fit to be tied."

"He promised to be good for one day." Julie looked up at her big, strong husband, thinking that she was the most blessed woman on earth. "Just today, mind you, and then he plans to fight fire with fire, he said."

Rafe shrugged. "Makes no difference to me." He glanced over to where the ladies of the Books'n'Bingo Society were fussing over Janet, Julianne and Judith—his three special-delivery valentines. "I'm living for the future these days."

"Me, too," Julie said, stepping up to the rose-festooned altar. This was heaven, all she'd ever dreamed of, all she'd ever wanted. After all the years of loving him from afar, finally Rafe Callahan would be her husband in name as well as spirit.

He looked down at her, smiling, and then sweetly kissed her lips before the priest had a chance to begin the service. The guests laughed again, enjoying their happiness, and Julie smiled. This was the start of their new lives together, a marriage reborn.

And then, like a benediction, the sound of hooves came to them. On the horizon, black shadow horses ran through the canyons, heralding blessed days ahead.

"Magic," Julie whispered to Rafe, and he nodded, holding her close.

True magic, the kind that would last forever.

Rancho Diablo magic.

* * * * *

HEART & HOME

Heartwarming romances where love can
happen right when you least expect it.

Harlequin®

American ★ Romance®

COMING NEXT MONTH
AVAILABLE FEBRUARY 14, 2012

#1389 ARIZONA COWBOY
Rodeo Rebels
Marin Thomas

#1390 RANCHER DADDY
Saddler's Prairie
Ann Roth

#1391 THE RODEO MAN'S DAUGHTER
Fatherhood
Barbara White Daille

#1392 THE DETECTIVE'S ACCIDENTAL BABY
Safe Harbor Medical
Jacqueline Diamond

*Louisa Morgan loves being around children.
So when she has the opportunity to tutor bedridden Ellie,
she's determined to bring joy back into the motherless
girl's world. Can she also help Ellie's father open his
heart again? Read on for a sneak peek of*

THE COWBOY FATHER

*by Linda Ford,
available February 2012 from Love Inspired Historical.*

Why had Louisa thought she could do this job? A bubble of self-pity whispered she was totally useless, but Louisa ignored it. She wasn't useless. She could help Ellie if the child allowed it.

Emmet walked her out, waiting until they were out of earshot to speak. "I sense you and Ellie are not getting along."

"Ellie has lost her freedom. On top of that, everything is new. Familiar things are gone. Her only defense is to exert what little independence she has left. I believe she will soon tire of it and find there are more enjoyable ways to pass the time."

He looked doubtful. Louisa feared he would tell her not to return. But after several seconds' consideration, he sighed heavily. "You're right about one thing. She's lost everything. She can hardly be blamed for feeling out of sorts."

"She hasn't lost everything, though." Her words were quiet, coming from a place full of certainty that Emmet was more than enough for this child. "She has you."

"She'll always have me. As long as I live." He clenched his fists. "And I fully intend to raise her in such a way that even if something happened to me, she would never feel like I was gone. I'd be in her thoughts and in her actions every day."

Peace filled Louisa. "Exactly what my father did."

Their gazes connected, forged a single thought about fathers and daughters…how each needed the other. How sweet the relationship was.

Louisa tipped her head away first. "I'll see you tomorrow."

Emmet nodded. "Until tomorrow then."

She climbed behind the wheel of their automobile and turned toward home. She admired Emmet's devotion to his child. It reminded her of the love her own father had lavished on Louisa and her sisters. Louisa smiled as fond memories of her father filled her thoughts. Ellie was a fortunate child to know such love.

Louisa understands what both father and daughter are going through. Will her compassion help them heal—and form a new family? Find out in
THE COWBOY FATHER
by Linda Ford, available February 14, 2012.

Love Inspired Books celebrates 15 years of inspirational romance in 2012! February puts the spotlight on Love Inspired Historical, with each book celebrating family and the special place it has in our hearts. Be sure to pick up all four Love Inspired Historical stories, available February 14, wherever books are sold.

Harlequin *Presents®*

USA TODAY bestselling author

Sarah Morgan

brings readers another enchanting story

ONCE A FERRARA WIFE...

When Laurel Ferrara is summoned back to Sicily by her estranged husband, billionaire Cristiano Ferrara, Laurel knows things are about to heat up. And Cristiano's power is a potent reminder of his Sicilian dynasty's unbreakable rule: once a Ferrara wife, always a Ferrara wife....

Sparks fly this February